TALES FROM THE FRINGES OF FEAR

TALES FROM THE FRINGES OF FEAR

JEFF SZPIRGLAS

ILLUSTRATED BY
STEVEN P. HUGHES

ORCA BOOK PUBLISHERS

Library and Archives Canada Cataloguing in Publication
Title: *Tales from the fringes of fear* / Jeff Szpirglas; illustrated by Steven P. Hughes.
Names: Szpirglas, Jeff, author. | Hughes, Steven P., 1989– illustrator.
Description: Short stories.
Identifiers: Canadiana (print) 20190169664 | Canadiana (ebook) 20190169818 |
ISBN 9781459824584 (softcover) | ISBN 9781459824591 (PDF) |
ISBN 9781459824607 (EPUB)
Classification: LCC PS8637.Z65 T36 2020 | DDC jC813/.6—dc23

Library of Congress Control Number: 2019947374
Simultaneously published in Canada and the United States in 2020

Summary: A collection of stories for middle readers that ranges from perplexing to petrifying.

Orca Book Publishers is committed to reducing the consumption of nonrenewable resources in the making of our books. We make every effort to use materials that support a sustainable future.

Orca Book Publishers gratefully acknowledges the support for its publishing programs provided by the following agencies: the Government of Canada, the Canada Council for the Arts and the Province of British Columbia through the BC Arts Council and the Book Publishing Tax Credit.

Edited by Tanya Trafford
Design by Dahlia Yuen
Illustrations and cover image by Steven P. Hughes
Author photo by Danielle Saint-Onge

ORCA BOOK PUBLISHERS
orcabook.com

Printed and bound in Canada.
23 22 21 20 • 4 3 2 1

FOR DANIELLE, RUBY, AND LÉO.
AND THE CATS!

CONTENTS

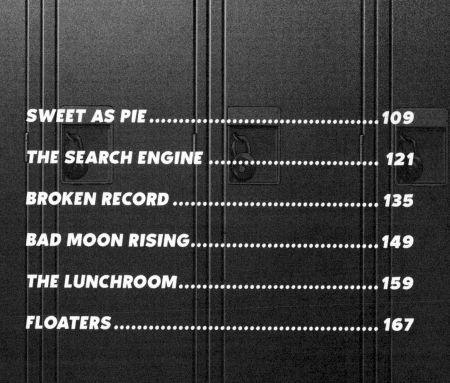

ERIN STAYS SHARP

Mr. Schmelp often made a clicking sound when he got angry or nervous. It sounded like he was somehow creating pressure using the roof of his mouth and the back of his throat, then pushing them close together until the two *click-click-clicked* away.

Today, Erin noted, Mr. Schmelp had been clicking incessantly.

Incessantly, she had learned (she sometimes read the dictionary for fun), meant doing something over and over again without stopping.

Schoolwork often bored Erin. If Mr. Schmelp instructed the class to do math exercises for a half hour, she would complete them in under ten. The same went for spelling, science and even social studies. That left plenty of time for her to sit and stare silently. Erin was an observer. She had noticed how many of the books in the classroom were about nature and animals (more than half), that Mr. Schmelp was missing a part of his ring finger and that he was pretty good at noticing when Erin had been observing things for too long.

Today Erin had been observing Mr. Schmelp incessantly.

Mr. Schmelp had been clicking his throat since 9:48 a.m. And he had paced around the room ten times. Erin had noted these behaviors in the past, but today there was something new to add to Schmelp's repertoire of tics. He kept glancing out the window to the parking lot outside.

With her exercises finished, Erin observed Mr. Schmelp further. She concentrated on his furtive glances. This wasn't just some unconscious act, like the clicking. These were deliberate peeks at the outside world. Erin wondered what he was looking for. All she could see through the grimy windows were the parking lot, the narrow road leading to the school and the woods on the other side of the road.

When the final bell rang, her classmates practically jumped out of their desks. Erin saw Mr. Schmelp glance out the window again and then make his way back to his own desk.

Erin picked up her things and left the classroom. She took her time walking down the hallway. When most of the students had left the building and some semblance of quiet had fallen again, she turned and started walking back toward Mr. Schmelp's classroom.

Most of the teachers were still in their classrooms, Erin observed, looking carefully into each one as she walked past the doorways. They were busy packing up, erasing blackboards or picking papers off the floor. All the doors were still open, except for Mr. Schmelp's, which was shut.

Almost.

The door was still open a crack. Erin decided to steal a peek to observe Mr. Schmelp's behavior.

He was sitting at his desk. He looked up now and again, mostly out the window, but he did not appear to notice Erin looking through the small opening.

Seeming satisfied that he was alone, Mr. Schmelp wrenched open the bottom drawer of his desk and pulled out a large canvas bag. Erin could see that the bag was zipped shut and fastened with a combination lock. Mr. Schmelp glanced out the window (again!), then undid the lock, unzipped the bag and inspected the contents within.

He placed the canvas bag on his lap and then took a pencil from his desk. Erin thought that was rather curious. She watched Mr. Schmelp lower the pencil toward the bag. She heard a metallic whirring sound. Very curious.

Something else caught Erin's attention. Through the window she spotted two black sedans pulling into the school parking lot. They were very shiny, with barely a speck of dirt on them. She was so busy thinking about how tough it must be to keep black cars clean that she failed to notice the door was slowly creaking open.

"Erin!" Mr. Schmelp exclaimed.

Erin jumped. "I'm sorry, Mr. Schmelp. I came back to—"

"What did you see?" he hissed.

Instinctively Erin pointed at the black cars outside.

Mr. Schmelp turned and followed her gaze. When he saw the cars, he flinched.

Something heavy clattered onto the floor, startling Erin. She briefly saw a metal object lying on the floor. Mr. Schmelp quickly scooped it up. Erin couldn't see anything behind the bulk of the teacher's desk, but she imagined that this object must have been in the canvas bag and was being shoved back inside. But why was Mr. Schmelp now on his hands and knees, staring at the floor with such a strange intensity?

"Mr. Schmelp? Er...can I help you with anything?"

Mr. Schmelp looked up at her. His face was panicky. "Quick, close the door!" he snapped.

"Did you drop something?" Erin asked, closing the door behind her and approaching the desk.

Mr. Schmelp didn't answer. He was too busy examining the floor.

Erin put down her backpack and tried to help, even though she had no idea what she was looking for. Whatever it was, Mr. Schmelp must have found it quickly. Erin saw a blur of motion, and then Mr. Schmelp was at the bag. He leaned over it, and she heard a *click*, as if something was being snapped shut, and then a *zip*.

Mr. Schmelp looked up, his brow coated with sweat. He looked exasperated and surprised to see Erin still standing there. He opened his mouth to speak, but the intercom buzzed.

"What is it?" he shouted at the little beige box.

A woman's voice crackled over the intercom. "There are some...*people*...to see you, Mr. Schmelp."

The teacher turned toward the window. The black sedans were parked right in front of the main doors. Their tinted windows made it impossible to see who might be inside. Mr. Schmelp gulped, then turned back to the intercom. "I'll b-be r-right there," he stuttered.

"Stay here," Mr. Schmelp said to Erin. "I'll be right back, and then we can talk." He quickly shuffled out of the room, slamming the door behind him.

With the coast clear, Erin took this opportunity to search Mr. Schmelp's desk. She yanked the bottom drawer open.

She pushed aside the crumpled papers and removed the bag. Through the canvas she could feel a heavy, box-shaped object. She shook it and heard something rattle. Erin took hold of the combination lock and stared at the numbers on the dial. If only Mr. Schmelp hadn't locked it, she thought, tugging at the mechanism. Then she could discover what all the fuss was about before he came back and—

Click.

In her hand, the lock had sprung open.

Mr. Schmelp had locked it but never spun the dial! Erin slowly unzipped the bag and reached inside.

"Huh?"

She was holding an electric pencil sharpener.

Erin turned the machine over in her hands, inspecting every side. But the sharpener yielded nothing of interest. The only notable feature was that the spinning blades and alcove for the shavings were hidden by dark-tinted plexiglass, like the windows of the sedans outside.

Also in the bag, Erin noted, were some books.

There were three in all, and they had been used thoroughly—broken spines, frayed pages, tattered corners. The covers were faded and torn, but Erin could still read the titles: *Exploring Entomology, Lermer's Guide to Costa Rican Wildlife, 2nd ed.* and *Endangered Fauna of Central America.*

She thumbed through the book about endangered species. Many pages were dog-eared. Passages were underlined. Notes were scrawled along the nearby margins. They must be Mr. Schmelp's observations and notes. But Erin did not have time to read through them right now. Her time would be better spent examining the sharpener.

Erin held it above her head to let some light pass through it, but the plexiglass casing revealed nothing. She was about to put it down again when she heard something inside the sharpener rattle. She peered into the interior through the small opening meant for pencils. She saw nothing.

Erin knew better than to stick her finger in there. She dashed back to her desk and grabbed a pencil. Only one way to find out what's inside, she told herself.

Erin jammed her pencil into the sharpener with such force that it snapped in half.

Frustrated, she held the broken end of the pencil before her like a lit stick of dynamite. She could feel her heart pounding in her chest.

She heard the sound of footsteps in the hallway. Someone was coming her way. Mr. Schmelp!

What would happen if she got caught? Probably detention for the rest of the month, if not the rest of the year! She was an A student. She could risk a mark on her record.

Erin grabbed the old books and shoved them back into the canvas bag. She picked up the lock from the table and slid the hook end through the loop at the end of the zipper. The footsteps were getting closer. She needed to get the broken piece of pencil out of the sharpener, and she needed to do it *now*. But there was no way to extract it without breaking the sharpener open, and that would only put her right back to square one and—

WHIRRRRRRRRRR!!!!

The sharpener spun madly, sucking in her pencil and chewing it to bits.

Impossible, Erin thought. An electric sharpener needed force on the pencil to work. She'd used one before. So how could this be?

No matter. With the evidence gone, Erin grabbed the sharpener, shoved it into the bag, zipped it up—

Erin heard the doorknob turn.

She snapped the lock into place, shoved the canvas bag into the desk drawer, then stepped away from the desk.

"Erin?" said Mr. Schmelp.

Erin flinched. She tucked the top half of the broken pencil into her pocket. "Y-yes, Mr. Schmelp?"

The silence that followed was so intense it nearly screamed.

Mr. Schmelp looked dazed. "Sorry to have kept you waiting." He stared out the window. Erin followed his gaze to the black sedans still parked outside. "You can go home now."

"But I thought you wanted to talk—"

"Just go," he told her, obviously preoccupied with the sedans. Erin noticed several figures climbing back into them. Then the sedans sped away, leaving a dusty trail behind them.

That night at home, Erin did what any good observer would do. She copied her notes from class into her diary. Here she had a master list of all Mr. Schmelp's tics, how much homework was assigned on a daily basis and the ratio of free time versus study time. Erin's diary was likely the best collection of notes ever recorded from classroom observance.

When she had finished, she pulled out her dad's nature encyclopedias from the bottom of her bookshelf. They were dusty from neglect, but Erin cracked them open and began to search for information. The books in Mr. Schmelp's bag had piqued her curiosity.

Costa Rica, she learned, had the most varied fauna of any country. More than 850 species of birds had been recorded, over 200 mammals, 35,000 insects—

Insects. Erin remembered that one of the books in Mr. Schmelp's bag had been about entomology, the study of bugs. She was on the right track.

She read and read, until her eyelids grew heavy. She put the books back onto their shelves and tumbled into bed.

WHIRRRRRRR...

Erin's eyes snapped open. She lay very still, not daring to shift her weight on the squeaky mattress. She knew that sound. It sounded just like—

WHIRRRR...

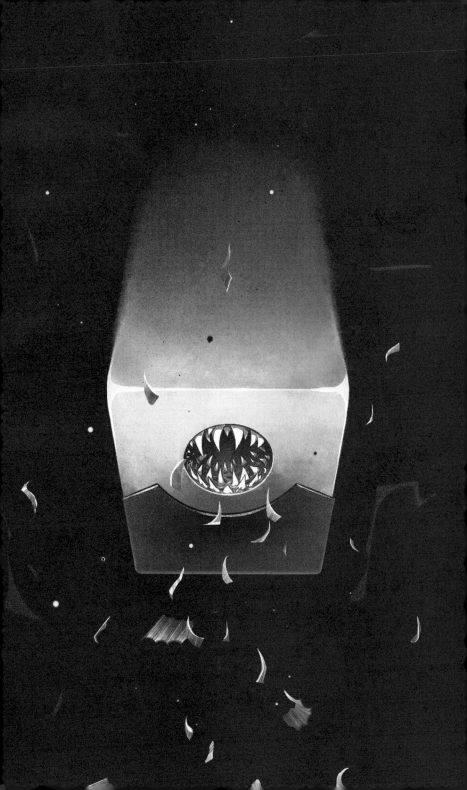

—just like the blades of Mr. Schmelp's pencil sharpener! But Erin had definitely put the sharpener back in Schmelp's bag. You didn't forget a detail like that.

A dream, she thought to herself. This is some stupid old—

WHIRRRRRRR….!

—dream?

Erin got out of bed. Her feet sunk into the thick carpet. Her ears were attuned like two satellite dishes on the sides of her head.

WHIRRRRRRR…

Erin flicked on the light.

She scanned her desk, her dresser and the floor around her for evidence of a disturbance. But nothing seemed out of place. And Erin was too keen an observer to make a mistake. Everything was in its place. Her closet door was closed all the way. Her books were stacked neatly on her desk. Her backpack's outside pocket was unzipped and open—

Erin remembered opening it to put her pencils away when she went back to Mr. Schmelp's class that afternoon. She was certain she had closed it before she walked home.

WHIRRRRR…

Erin gasped.

There on her desk lay a small pile of wooden shavings.

Cautiously Erin approached. She dipped her index finger into the shaving pile and lifted the finger to her face for closer inspection. The shavings were clumped together and a bit wet.

WHIRRRR…

Erin spun around. The wooden leg of a doll on the far shelf had been reduced to dust. Erin paced to the other side of the room and stuck another finger into the shaved remains. They were wet too.

WHIRRRRRRRRRRRRRRRRRR...

The whirring continued. Erin dropped to her knees, her ears locking onto the source of the sound. She pushed her night table aside. There, in the wooden baseboard, she noticed a small hole—a hole about the size of the one on Mr. Schmelp's pencil sharpener.

The whirring continued. Erin jumped up, grabbed a pencil from her desk and raced back to the wall. She jammed her pencil into the hole.

WHIRRRRRRRRRR!!!!!!

The pencil shuddered in Erin's sweaty palm. She wrenched it out of the baseboard and was shocked to discover it was now just a stub. Only the eraser end and enough wood to create a sharpened point were left.

After a moment of silence, the whirring started again. Wide-eyed, Erin dropped the remains of her pencil and backed away.

The next day Erin kept a close eye on Mr. Schmelp. As he had the day before, he seemed on edge, constantly twitching, only now he was no longer searching out the window for cars. His eyes were constantly scanning the corners of the room. He kept returning to the box of pencils by the sharpener, inspecting them like an expert might inspect diamonds. Erin wasn't sure why she hadn't told him yet what had happened the previous night. She knew the events in the classroom and in her bedroom yesterday were connected. She just didn't know how. More observing was required.

All morning Erin followed Mr. Schmelp's unusual movements, watching as he stopped speaking to the class in midsentence, as if listening to some far-off sound. Erin soon found herself searching the room too, because she was starting to suspect she knew what Mr. Schmelp was searching for.

Suddenly the teacher walked up to her desk. A scrap of paper fluttered down directly over her spiral coiled notebook.

It was a note.

SEE ME AT 3:30, it read.

Erin looked up. Mr. Schmelp was staring down at her, nodding.

Erin was a wreck. She pulled at her hair, gnawed her pencil, had a slight coughing fit and bit a few nails waiting for three thirty to arrive. Her eyes, which would normally be tracking her peers and their activities, were darting this way and that. When the bell finally rang, Mr. Schmelp gave her a business-like glance.

Erin remained in her seat as the rest of her classmates got up to go.

Now it was just Erin, Mr. Schmelp and the silence.

Mr. Schmelp sat at his desk and cracked his knuckles. Enhanced by the surrounding silence, the knuckle-cracking seemed louder than an earthquake.

"I know you know," Mr. Schmelp said finally.

"You know I know what?"

"You *know* what I know you know," he said. He stood up, stormed over to Erin and slammed his pencil sharpener down on top of her desk. He did it with such force that the black casing cracked.

"You broke it," Erin gasped.

Mr. Schmelp shook his head and then ripped off the plexiglass casing. Erin looked down and saw that it was empty, only a few wooden shavings inside. Blades for sharpening pencils were nowhere to be seen. "There was nothing to break," he told her.

"Then what was it I heard jiggling—" Erin began.

Busted! Now he knows I know! she thought.

"What you heard *jiggling*," said Mr. Schmelp, "is a very unique species of insect. Because of the protective shield on the sharpener, you surmised that there were blades within. You wouldn't be far from the truth. The creature that until very recently had been living in that mock sharpener has a set of spinning mandibles. They can whirl as fast as the blades of a food processor. They're sharp enough to slice into the side of a tree as if it were a stalk of celery—"

"Sounds dangerous," said Erin.

Mr. Schmelp nodded. Then he held out his hand and wiggled his fingers. Up close, Erin could see that his ring finger ended not with flesh and fingernail but with an awkward stump. So *that's* what had happened to it! thought Erin.

"It can be," said Mr. Schmelp, and then he sighed. "It's not a flesh-eater, strictly speaking. What happened to me was purely a defensive tactic. At least, that's what I have come to believe."

"They're not from around here, are they?" Erin asked. She was trying hard not to think about her bedroom and what it might look like when she got home. She realized now that somehow this creature must have made its way into her bag yesterday.

"I found one this past summer while vacationing in the cloud forests of Monteverde, Costa Rica."

Erin's eyes lit up. "The books—"

"Contained my notes and observations," Mr. Schmelp finished. "Before I settled into a life of teaching, I was a naturalist. Unfortunately for me, nature doesn't pay the bills. But if I could sell a certain endangered animal on the black market...well...let's just say there would be money to burn."

"Why are you telling me this?"

"Because you're going to have to help me find it!" Mr. Schmelp barked. "I know you're quite the observer, Erin. But so am I. Perhaps you are not aware of this, but I have observed *you* over the course of the year. Your notes are quite thorough. And your skills are most impressive. Now you are going to have to put them to use."

"What do you want?"

"I want that creature back."

"I don't have it." While this was technically true, Erin knew she was keeping information from Mr. Schmelp, and she wasn't sure why.

"I was afraid you were going to say that." Mr. Schmelp clicked nervously.

"Why? What's so important about some dumb bug with an eating disorder?"

"You remember those men who came here yesterday? The ones in the black cars?"

Erin nodded.

"They work for the government. It seems I'm not the only one who managed to bring one of those insects home. And it seems I'm not the only one who may have…misplaced one."

"What's your point?"

Mr. Schmelp leaned in close to Erin now. "Do you know why those creatures became endangered in the first place?"

Erin wiped the spit from her face. "Destruction of the environment? Depletion of the ozone layer?"

Mr. Schmelp shook his head. "The Costa Rican government issued a law to have them destroyed. Those little critters are wood-eaters. They're worse than a hundred plagues of locusts unleashed at once. They'll bore through every wooden thing in their path. It's one thing to have them living in a dense cloud forest, where there's constant growth. Here, things are different, and the insects are considerably more dangerous. The one the government is looking for is male. Mine is female. If those two ever got together…"

Erin nodded, then got up from her desk to put her coat on. "I think I know where it might be. I'll start looking right away."

Flashlight in hand, Erin moved the night table and inspected the wooden hole in the baseboard. She pointed the flashlight at the opening, then slowly inched toward the hole.

As tempting as it was, she refrained from putting her finger in the hole. She tapped the side of the baseboard. The wall behind felt hollow, like the insides had been scooped out.

And there was something else too. She could feel something jiggle when she tapped the wall. Perhaps it was a loose wire. Or a stray piece of drywall.

Perhaps.

Erin moved closer still. If something had burrowed its way down inside, how would she get it out now?

Erin reached forward to tap the baseboard again.

"Ouch!" she yelped, dropping the flashlight. She clasped a palm around her left index finger. A small pearl of blood formed on the pad of the fingertip. A sliver of wood was lodged underneath the skin.

Erin sucked the blood away, then brought the thumb and index finger of her right hand together like makeshift tweezers. She grabbed hold of the sharp end of the sliver with the edges of her fingernails and pulled.

"Aaaah!" she yelped. There was another bead of blood.

The sliver, Erin could see, was more significant than she'd first imagined. Although she had wrenched out a long chunk, most of the wood was still buried in her fingertip.

Erin was trying to pull the rest out when the splinter sticking out of her finger suddenly curled and arched like the tail of a scorpion. Then, ever so slowly, it began to ease itself back into Erin's finger.

Erin opened her mouth to scream, but another sound came first.

WHIRRRRRRRRRRRRRRRRRR.......!

THE HIBERNACULUM

Caleb stepped off the bus and was slapped in the face by a cold burst of winter air. Why they had to go on a field trip in the middle of January was beyond him, yet here they were.

His teacher, Ms. Wynne, didn't look particularly pleased about being here either. She was currently busy texting something on her cell phone. Maybe just searching for a signal. The class had been bused to this outdoor education center on the outer edge of the school district, somewhere between the farmers' fields and the scrubby wilderness.

Now the whole class stood at the edge of a small wooded area. Behind them a large transport truck roared across the small strip of snowy road that disappeared into the winter landscape. The rush of air in its wake only bit harder at exposed skin.

In front of them stood an old schoolhouse. It had been standing there for a hundred years—at least, that's what Ms. Wynne had told them.

Caleb and the rest of the class stood shivering as a door creaked open and a man stepped out. He was tall and bearded and dressed much better for the weather than any of the students were. He introduced himself as Jack, the outdoor education instructor. He didn't seem to care how uncomfortable the students seemed to be in the frigid environment. "A walk outside will do you all some good," he said. "Put your things inside, and we'll get started."

Jack had given the class only a brief respite from the cold. The inside of the ancient schoolhouse had been kept in its original condition, aside from new electrical outlets that allowed for some space heaters. Caleb couldn't figure out how Jack kept himself warm. Maybe it was his thick beard or the massive woolen cap that covered his head of equally thick, almost wiry hair. Even with the heaters, the schoolhouse was too cold inside for the students to take off their winter gear. Jack didn't give them any time for that anyway.

In a few moments the class was ushered back outside and onto a small path behind the schoolhouse that snaked into the woods.

Caleb soon found himself near the back of the line, behind even Ms. Wynne, who was still trying to find a cell signal. Jack was way up ahead, at the front of the single-file line. Caleb could hear Jack droning on about the different birds and animals that could survive the winter months, but the chatter from the rest of his peers and the crunching of boots in snow made it impossible for him to fully register everything Jack said.

And, as they often did, Caleb's eyes and mind began to wander.

He gazed through the thick canopy of trees, looking up at the dark greens of the conifers, noting how snow-covered the branches were and wondering how anything could survive the long winter.

Caleb lowered his head and scanned the forest. He spotted something in the distance, behind a row of pine trees. The group ahead of him was moving at a snail's pace, and if there was one thing Caleb hated, it was waiting in line.

He stepped off the path, enjoying the sound of his boots crunching through the frozen top layer of snow. It was ankle-deep, and he had to steady himself to keep from pitching over. He looked back and determined that nobody had noticed his leaving. Didn't matter if they had—this was a field trip, and he was exploring. Wasn't that the point?

Caleb thumped ahead, past the pines and into a clearing, and there it was. A large heap of rocks and crisscrossed branches jutting out at strange angles. The mound was about the size a school bus, if a bus had suddenly become petrified and fragmented and then collapsed onto the ground in the middle of the woods. What the heck was it?

Not natural, Caleb determined. This was something a person had made. He probed his way around the mound of rocks. He noticed the odd cinder block here or there, which only proved his theory that someone had dumped this heap of refuse here. Which raised the question, Why dump it here? What was the point?

For the first time on this whole trip, Caleb found himself interested and curious. He was about to double back and share his discovery when a voice startled him from behind. "Ah, I see you've found the hibernaculum."

Caleb jumped, lost his balance and fell butt first into the snow.

There was a chorus of laughter, and when Caleb whipped his head back around, he saw the rest of the class gathered there, as if they'd been waiting for him the whole time.

Jack reached out a meaty hand and clasped Caleb's wrist. Caleb found himself heaved back onto his feet. He stumbled backward unsteadily until he was part of the crowd of students.

"I'd be careful around the hibernaculum," Jack said matter-of-factly.

"The *what*?" a girl named Kate piped up from somewhere in the crowd.

Jack turned to the group and began lecturing. "*Hibernaculum*. It's a structure many animals take refuge in during the cold winter months. Bears, bats...or in this case, something that can easily wriggle into the small gaps between the rocks."

"Worms?" Kate suggested.

There were a few giggles, but Jack silenced the class with a quick slash of his hand. The dude was intense.

"You're closer than you think. But worms don't need a cave. They're already most at home buried under the earth. However, our friendly local garter snakes? Burrowing is not as easy for them to do."

At the word *snakes*, Caleb noticed a divided reaction among his classmates. Some took a step back from the rocks, while others leaned in with curiosity and newfound interest.

"We built this for a reason," Jack continued. "Across the highway there was a construction crew tearing down an old farmhouse that had been abandoned twenty years earlier. Thing is, once the bulldozer had knocked it down, they looked into the basement and found that snakes had been brumating there over the winter."

"Don't you mean hibernating?" Kate tried. "Because, like you said, it's a hibernate-u-lem."

"Hibernaculum," Jack corrected, "and no. Brumating is what snakes do. They and other cold-blooded reptiles can't afford to hibernate. They'd freeze to death. Instead, their metabolic rates slow, but they still have just enough energy to take turns moving in and out of the center of their nest ball. To keep warm."

"A nest *ball*? Gross!" cried Kate.

But this was fascinating to Caleb. "How many snakes are in a nest?" he asked.

"In this case, probably seven or eight hundred—"

Someone, probably Kate, let out an audible gag.

"That's nothing." Jack smiled, seeming to enjoy the reaction he was getting. "In ssssome parts around here, the snakes will congregate into big, slithering balls of several *thousand*."

Over the buzz of students expressing horror, Caleb spoke aloud to himself. "To keep warm…"

"Exactly," Jack replied. "Snakes are ectotherms. They don't produce their own body heat. So in the winter months, they gather in these hibernaculums, below the frost line, in huge balls, taking turns keeping warm by moving from the outside of the ball to the middle. It's quite amazing, if you think about it."

Caleb leaned closer to the mound. "How did you get them to use this hibernaculum instead?"

"The snakes were going to be destroyed. So we dug a new pit, put these rocks and branches over it, and brought the snakes over to our outdoor education center. It's quite a good spot for them, away from the roar of the road, don't you think?"

They spent the rest of the day playing around in the snow, recreating how the children of a hundred years ago would have experienced a winter day. There was a failed attempt at snowshoeing and an impromptu snowball fight that ended almost as soon as it had begun and resulted in at least one bloody nose.

Caleb actually found himself enjoying the outdoor education center, in spite of the cold. There was something eerily calm about the place, if you could ignore the occasional roar of trucks along the road in the distance and the constant hubbub of the other students.

So when it was time to go back to the schoolhouse and pack up their things, Caleb decided to give the nearby surroundings one last look.

He wandered around behind the schoolhouse, close to where they'd started their initial journey into the forest. He noticed something in the underbrush.

It was another rock pile—or something akin to one.

Caleb stepped closer and realized that these rocks had not been dumped here but were instead held together by concrete. The structure was under the thick lower branches of a pine tree, hidden from view.

He knew exactly what it was. A well.

It clearly had not been used for some time. When the schoolhouse was actually still a school, people probably used the well to draw up water—from an underground stream maybe? But now that the building was equipped with pipes and running water, the well was no longer necessary.

Still, Caleb found it curious that Jack hadn't pointed out the well during the tour. It was a perfect symbol of the olden days. Caleb took another step closer and then heard a crackling beneath his feet. He felt the ground beneath him give way.

Caleb hit the ground with a heavy thud that sent shock waves through his bones. His jaw snapped shut and his teeth clacked together loudly. Pain flared through his body. Caleb winced, waiting for the sensation to dissipate. He tried moving his legs and arms, and although they still throbbed from the sudden impact, he was pretty sure nothing was broken. He came to this conclusion mainly because he was able to stand up without screaming.

Now came the trickier part. How to get the heck out of here. He was in darkness, but the echo from his fall suggested this was a big space.

Caleb looked up. A shaft of light punched through the dark, falling on the wall across from him. The jagged rocks illuminated by the one bit of daylight told Caleb he was in some kind of cavern. This wasn't a well. "Help!" he screamed, and although his voice bounced around the walls, he could tell it wasn't going to carry all the way up to the opening he'd fallen through.

Now he began to worry.

"It's okay," he told himself, wrapping his arms around his torso. The cavern wasn't as cold as the winter landscape above him, but it was still chilly. "They're not going to leave without you. They're going to have to call somebody. Jack will know where to look." But trying to reassure himself wasn't working.

So he stood there—for how long he wasn't sure—looking, listening, waiting.

In the dark and stillness of the cavern, Caleb thought he heard far-off voices. They were faint and thin. Was it Ms. Wynne and the others? Again, he told himself, they wouldn't leave without him.

As long as he stayed here, near the opening, he would be fine.

Eventually somebody would start to poke around. Somebody would discover the opening. Somebody would lower a rope, and then he would be safe.

Besides, Jack would know what to do.

Jack.

"Jack!" Caleb tried again, at the top of his lungs. The sound reverberated around the cavern. "Jack, I'm here!"

He screamed again, loudly. Even though he knew it was hopeless, he continued to yell for a minute, maybe two. Maybe even three. The vapor from his breath piped out in staccato bursts.

Eventually Caleb stopped. His throat was sore and raw. His lungs hurt. He sat down and took some deep breaths.

There was silence again.

It occurred to him that the cavern was perhaps deeper than the hibernaculum Jack had created for those garter snakes. He had no sense of space down here, even as his eyes began to adjust to his dimly lit surroundings. How far had he fallen? Ten feet? Twenty?

And then Caleb *did* hear a sound.

It wasn't coming from above. The sound was slight but clear. It was coming from down here in the cavern, somewhere behind him.

He stood up again, his breath jagged.

He turned, trying to source the sound.

It grew louder. Or closer. He couldn't tell.

The sound was not dirt settling. It was definitely something approaching. An animal perhaps?

Caleb's immediate fear was that it was some large, dangerous animal, but this sound suggested something small. A badger? Rats even? He didn't want to encounter whatever was coming his way, but he felt confident that he was the largest animal around. He could defend himself.

Still, most animals, having heard the screaming of a boy, would have turned and fled the other way. This one kept coming closer.

Caleb tightened his hands into fists. Then he opened them and clapped loudly, so the echo would come suddenly, startlingly.

He waited for the loud sound to fade, hoping he'd stopped the thing from coming closer.

Yet he could still hear it, even closer now.

Caleb backed up. He cocked his head up into the light. "Help! There's something down here!" he shouted urgently.

"Yesssss," a voice hissed from behind.

Caleb heard a high-pitched shriek. It took him a second to realize it was his own.

He whipped around.

"Jack?" Caleb said, trying to register the form moving toward him in the near-darkness. He'd been staring at Jack all day. He'd recognize the man's gait and movements.

Of *course* it was Jack, Caleb realized, letting out a sigh of relief. Jack knew these caves. He'd built the hibernaculum, for goodness' sake. He'd figured out that Caleb had fallen through and was here to rescue him.

"Jack, I fell...I was so worried," Caleb said, his voice shaky, close to breaking.

But Jack was silent. And he kept coming closer, the sound of his breath hissy and raspy, like he, too, had been injured from falling through a hole in the ground.

"Sssssstay there," he said.

Caleb backed away. "Jack?"

Jack stepped into the shaft of light coming from above, and Caleb *saw*.

Not Jack!

No, no, no…

The thing before him resembled a man only in the barest sense. The misshapen form had what you might call legs and arms and a head, but its features kept shifting. Wriggling even. Coming apart and then fusing together again.

Camouflage.

Down here Jack didn't need camouflage.

That pile of rubble dumped in the middle of the woods—that was no hibernaculum. That was the facade to fool everyone. The hibernaculum was here. The snakes were here. They were moving in a ball, lifting and pushing and tightening and coiling until they turned themselves into something that looked almost human.

How they had fooled everyone above, Caleb did not know.

"That'ssss right," Jack said.

How could they even use language? They were just snakes. A writhing mass of snakes.

"Impossible," Caleb said.

"Not ssssssnakesssss," the voice of the thing—*things*—said.

Caleb squinted to get a better look. These weren't just common garter snakes. They had scales, of course. And they were legless. But that's where the similarities stopped.

Snakes couldn't blink their eyes, but these ones did. And snakes couldn't change their color like these things could.

The creatures, whatever they were, began to slither and twist, dismantling the humanoid body they'd assembled. Caleb could see how they lengthened, thickening their girth or drawing themselves into spidery thin lines as they oozed from one object into many slithering beasts. They looked more like something you'd find under the sea, like the tentacles of a hundred writhing octopuses come to life.

They reached Caleb's feet.

And began to wrap around them.

Caleb opened his mouth to scream, and that's when they made their move, slithering quickly up the sides of his body and into the open orifice.

"There you are!" said Ms. Wynne, looking relieved.

Caleb had a dazed expression on his face.

Ms. Wynne was standing in front of the school bus. Everybody else was inside. Many of his classmates had their faces pressed against the frosted windows, pointing and making faces.

Caleb ignored them.

He stared dead ahead.

"We were worried. We were just about to call the police."

Caleb nodded.

Ms. Wynne shook her head. "Did Jack send you over here? I made him go and look for you."

"Yesssss," Caleb said with a smile. "He ssssertainly did."

Ms. Wynne raised an eyebrow. "You're sure you're okay?"

Caleb looked at the bus and nodded.

"Good. It's freezing out here. Let's get on the bus and get back to school. It's much warmer there."

Caleb could not agree more. They were going someplace much, much warmer. And with an ample food supply for the winter months.

It would almost be like some kind of vacation.

DETENTION

Tick, tick, tick went the clock on the wall.

Jill stared at it. It was one of those circular clocks that marks the minutes and seconds, but she was certain it wasn't keeping up with real time. Maybe school clocks moved at their own speed. Maybe it was only because Jill was in recess detention.

Jill wasn't even sure why she and Priyanka were in trouble. She had only been whispering to her friend about what they were going to do after school. They hadn't even raised their voices like Tyler Price always did, and he *never* had to stay in for recess! Besides, *everyone* whispered when Mr. Lee was in the middle of a lesson. That's what happened when teachers were boring.

Still, here they were, just the two of them—three, if you counted Mr. Lee. He just sat at his desk, reading a newspaper, while that clock kept ticking.

Mr. Lee put the paper down and stared at them with a piercing gaze. Jill wondered if he'd studied hypnosis before becoming a teacher.

Jill looked at Priyanka. Priyanka looked at Jill and shrugged.

Tick, tick, tick went the clock.

"Time's up," Mr. Lee said, nearly leaping out of his seat, giving the clock one final glance and then opening the door for them. He motioned to the empty hallway. "I trust you'll remember to use proper manners in my class next time," he said.

"Uh...sure thing, Mr. Lee," Priyanka muttered. Jill was staring at Mr. Lee. Priyanka grabbed her friend by the arm and dragged her into the hallway.

Only when they were out of the classroom and making their way to the playground did Jill manage to shake her head and get rid of the haze she had been floating in.

"That took forever," she said with a huff.

"Totally," agreed Priyanka. "I bet there's probably only, like, five minutes of break time left."

"I'll take it," Jill said, pushing the door open and stepping outside. She closed her eyes and let the warm sunshine hit her face.

"Jill," Priyanka gasped.

Jill felt Priyanka's hand tighten on her wrist. Priyanka was looking around the playground, a worried expression on her face.

"What is it?" Jill asked.

But before Priyanka could respond, Jill understood. There should have been kids here, running around, screaming, shooting hoops. But the playground was empty.

And quiet.

"Did we miss the bell?" Jill asked.

"It must have rung before we got outside," Priyanka said. "And we missed it. How could we miss a thing like that? And why didn't we hear the rest of the students going back inside?"

"I don't know," Jill said, "but we must have. There's no other explanation. That's probably exactly what Mr. Lee planned. Very funny. But we'd better get to class before he gives us *another* detention."

The two girls did an about-face, opened the door and scurried back down the hall, which also was strangely empty.

When Jill opened the door to her classroom, the one she and Priyanka had been sitting in just minutes earlier, she saw the students all working quietly at their desks. "What the—?"

How had they come in so quickly?

And why were they working so quietly?

As before, Mr. Lee was sitting at his desk, reading the newspaper, almost as if he'd been waiting for the girls to come right back with confused looks on their faces. The rest of the students were busy scribbling notes from the board into their workbooks.

"Ha, some joke," Jill huffed under her breath. "Good one, getting us to miss that recess bell."

She marched down the aisle toward her desk, still thinking about Mr. Lee and what he had done. She turned and tried to slide into her chair.

"Whoa! What are you doing?"

Jill jumped back, eyes wide.

There was a boy sitting at her desk. And it wasn't anybody she recognized. What was he doing here? Didn't he realize that this wasn't his classroom and this wasn't his desk? Did he need Jill to spell it out for him? Apparently so. "This is *my* seat," Jill said sharply.

The boy, whose eyes were as wide as Jill's, raised his hand. "Mr. Lee," he called. "Who *is* this? Did we get a new student or something?"

As Jill opened her mouth to inform this kid, whoever he was, that he was in the wrong place, she noticed that the entire class was full of students who had stumbled into the wrong room.

With the exception of Priyanka, who still stood by the door, looking like she'd seen a ghost, the students were all complete strangers.

Mr. Lee looked up from his paper. "Come here, girls," he said softly but firmly.

Jill moved away from the impostor at her desk and met Priyanka by their teacher's desk. "Mr. Lee, this is ridiculous," she said. "I told you we were sorry. We won't talk out of turn in your class again, I *promise*."

"Really we won't," Priyanka added. "But what the heck is going on here?"

Mr. Lee stared at the two intently for a long moment. He opened his mouth to speak. And then he flipped up the newspaper so that it formed a barrier between him and the girls.

"Mr. Lee?"

"Shhh," he said, turning the pages. "I'm reading. You should be too."

The newspaper headline indicated something about a war "raging" over in Europe. That was weird. There wasn't any war in Europe that Jill could recall.

"Go to the library," Mr. Lee said, lowering the paper.

"Huh?"

"The *library*, Jill. You'll find the answers you seek there."

With that Mr. Lee flipped the paper back up. Jill stared at him—or, rather, at the newspaper, the one with a headline that made no sense. Then her eyes darted to the corner of the page where the date was printed. The day and the month were today's, but the year? It was ten years ahead! Must be a misprint, she decided. What else could it be?

"Come on, Jill," Priyanka said, grabbing her and yanking her away from Mr. Lee's desk. "This has gone far enough. Let's go talk to the principal."

Out in the hallway, Jill looked at her surroundings more closely. The school hadn't changed, but some of the details had. Like the framed photographs of the graduating classes. For starters, there were more of them lining the wall than before. It wasn't a detail you'd notice unless you were looking for things that didn't belong.

Jill slowed down, leaving Priyanka to make her way to the office alone.

She scanned the grad pictures. A mosaic of student photographs stared back at her: head shots of students against the same dull-blue background. She saw her older brother in one of the photos. He'd graduated two years back, but...

What was it that didn't fit?

Jill stepped back, eyeing the images, taking them in. There were pictures of all the graduating classes, including next year's group of students. *They were already up on the wall.* And the year after that, and the year after that…Those kids couldn't have graduated yet, so why were their pictures hanging here?

Jill stopped when she recognized some students from her grade.

There they were, all looking older, all staring at her from the photograph. Everyone except for Priyanka and Jill, who were nowhere to be seen.

Mr. Lee's photo, of course, was there too. He stared out with eyes that seemed to recognize Jill.

Jill stepped back, shaking her head. "It's impossible," she breathed.

She studied the pictures of the group of students a year younger than her. There *they* were, all grown up, all graduated, and there was Mr. Lee, looking exactly the same.

She flipped her gaze from this picture of Mr. Lee to the one taken with her grade.

They were nearly identical.

She kept retracing her steps, staring at the grad photos, each class picture taking her back one year in time. She stared intently at Mr. Lee's image in each ensemble. Backward she went, one year after another. She went back ten years, twenty years, her heart beginning to thud more heavily as she focused on the photographs of her teacher.

It was the *same* picture of him every year.

"Jill?" said someone standing directly behind her.

Jill screamed.

It was only Priyanka, but Jill was already spooked to the core.

"Sorry, Jilly! I didn't mean to scare you. There was no one in the office. Which is weird."

With a shaky hand, Jill pointed out the photographs to Priyanka. "Mr. Lee hasn't *aged*," she said, still not fully understanding her own discovery. She pulled Priyanka all the way down to the other end of the hall. Back thirty-five years, and there he was again. "See? The same man, the same face!"

Priyanka saw. The clues had been there all this time, all these years.

"Do we go back? Tell him we know?" Priyanka asked.

Jill dug into her pocket and pulled out her cell phone. "I'm calling my mom," she said, keying in a number. But the phone wouldn't connect.

She tried again, her dad's number this time.

No connection.

She tried to find a Wi-Fi signal in the school, but the phone wouldn't respond.

Neither would Priyanka's.

"I always get the best signal right near those big windows at the back of the library," Priyanka said.

Jill's heart skipped a beat. "He *wanted* us to go to the library," she said, mostly to herself. "He wanted us to read."

"We could read *anywhere*," Priyanka mused.

"Maybe he wanted us to find something specific," Jill said.

The library was empty and quiet, which is what Mrs. Mosher, the cranky old librarian, always told the students she wanted. It was almost the same kind of quiet you get in one of those soundproof rooms, except for the clock on the wall above Mrs. Mosher's desk, ticking off the seconds.

Mrs. Mosher was not at her desk or anywhere by the shelves, the only other place you were likely to find her. Maybe she'd slipped off for a bathroom break or something.

Tick, tick, tick went the clock. Priyanka and Jill scanned the room, each of them almost afraid to break the strange silence pulsing through the place.

Out of the corner of her eye Jill saw a ruffle of movement. A girl of about their age emerged from behind one of the library stacks. She was looking intently at the shelves, a small pile of books in her arms. But instead of pulling books off shelves, she was putting them on.

"Maybe she's one of Mrs. Mosher's volunteers," Priyanka said, her voice loud enough to catch the girl's attention.

"Oh, hey there! What class are you coming from?" asked the girl.

"Mr. Lee's," Priyanka said.

The girl narrowed her eyes. She put the rest of the books down on the cart beside her. She took a few steps closer to the girls. "But they aren't expected here until third period tomorrow."

"Wow, you sure know the library schedule," Priyanka said.

The girl stopped and shrugged. Then her eyes opened wide. "Oh, *I* get it. You're *the two*," she said mysteriously.

Priyanka and Jill exchanged uneasy glances. "The two?"

"Mr. Lee told me he was going to keep a couple in for detention. Ergo, you must be the two."

"*Ergo?*"

"It's Latin, another word for *therefore*. Don't you learn *anything* in this place?" The girl moved over to a small table by Mrs. Mosher's desk, flipped open a book laying there and started reading.

This girl sure talked weird, but Jill was focused on more pressing matters. "Why would Mr. Lee tell you about giving us a detention?"

"You're making it sound like he planned the whole detention ahead of time," Priyanka added.

"Of course he did," the girl said with a smile. She looked at the clock on the wall above Mrs. Mosher's desk. It looked exactly like the one in Mr. Lee's room. And its second hand ticked along in the same jerky manner, moving across the dial in the same slow, deliberate spurts that didn't feel remotely like seconds.

Jill rushed over to the girl and grabbed her by the sleeve. "I don't know who you are, but if you're in on this joke with Mr. Lee, it's gone far enough. What is going on around here?"

That's when Jill noticed the book the girl was reading. It was an old, leather-bound volume that seemed more ancient than any book she'd ever seen. The leather was cracked and flaking, the pages yellow with age. The book had been opened to a spread with an image of an old-fashioned clock.

Kind of like the one up on the wall, actually.

The illustration had wavy lines radiating out from the clock and wrapping around smaller images of a person.

A person who seemed to be trying to run or pull away from the clock, if you used your imagination.

A series of mathematical formulas was inked on the page, along with words in a language Jill couldn't place. Italian? Latin?

She suddenly felt dizzy.

All that filled her head now was the sound of the clock ticking.

"Sorry," the girl said, jerking out of Jill's grip and focusing on the book. "I need to get back to my reading. Trying to brush up on my skills. I haven't used them in some time, but I was feeling a bit old and needed...some refreshment."

Priyanka nudged Jill. "Check out what she's wearing."

Jill saw what she meant. There was something about the girl's clothes that didn't seem right. They were a completely different style than hers and Priyanka's—a style neither of them would be caught dead in. Come to think of it, they were the kind of clothes you'd find on an older woman like Mrs. Mosher, wherever she was. And by the way they hung off the girl's body, Jill figured they were sized for an adult, not a kid.

Jill looked around the library. There had to be someone here who could help them. "Mrs. Mosher!" she called. Jill moved over to the desk where the cranky old librarian had always sat, watching them from behind her thick-rimmed glasses.

But the world around her was swimming. The clock's ticks had magnified to gong-like poundings, each one making her head blur in and out of consciousness.

In and out, and in and out, and...

Tick, tick, tick went the clock on the wall.

Jill opened her eyes. The world was still blurring at the edges but gradually coming into focus.

She blinked again, and her vision filled with the image of a clock. She stared at the hands. It was one fifteen. Cripes! Had she been sleeping for two hours already?

Wait a minute! *Sleeping*? She bolted upright when she realized she was lying down in the library.

Well, it looked like the library. It was the same space, and there was a desk at the front of the room, and there was that same clock on the wall above it, only…

Only now the shelves of books looked different, like they hadn't been filled with books at all but with rows of small, thin pieces of metal.

Jill shook the foggy feeling out of her head and got up to stagger toward the shelves.

Priyanka was standing by one, pulling pieces of metal from it, clearly confused. "What happened to all the books?"

Jill stopped at the closest shelf and grabbed one of the thin slivers of metal. There were no words on it, just a series of letters and numbers across the front, like a code.

"Oh, I see you noticed the change," a voice called out from behind them.

Jill turned to find the girl who'd been reading the old leather-bound book.

"They outlawed books, but I think you missed *that* part. This is the only reading we have nowadays, I'm afraid.

You were out for two hours. So that adds up to...what? Over 150 years."

Jill threw down the metal plate and stormed toward the girl. "What did you do to us? You started to read from that book, and then everything went spinny, and—"

"I tried to find a friend, you see. I tried it first with Albert Lee. But he wouldn't stay young. He got tired of it. Can you believe that? He *wanted* to get older. He still stayed here, of course. Nobody who gets pulled through the years ever wants to truly grow old."

"So you're saying you can manipulate time?"

"Yes. If you use the right clock and follow the instructions, you can stay young forever," the girl said, motioning to the book and then to the clock above Mrs. Mosher's desk.

"Time is life, but what is life without friends?" the girl continued. "Albert said he was going to find some friends for me, and that's just what he delivered. He had to, you see. Because I was the one who put him on detention in the first place. He owes me!"

Jill shook her head. "You put *him* on detention? You're just a kid."

The girl smiled, reached into the pocket of her sweater and pulled out a pair of thick, old glasses. Mrs. Mosher's glasses, to be precise. "Funny, that. I'm not entirely sure how it works, to be honest, how I can skip ahead and somehow get time back, but I know I don't need *these* anymore. And you can stay young like me too, if you desire."

Jill and Priyanka backed away from the girl. As they looked around, they noticed more details about the library. The windows were actually strange pieces of glass that radiated light instead of showing what was outside. The ceiling was covered with screens broadcasting images from all around the school, like a massive security system.

"This is impossible," Jill muttered. She tracked movement on one of the screens. A man bolted out of the office and ran down the hallway toward the library. A man she recognized.

The door burst open.

It was Mr. Lee, and he was shaking. He stared at them, eyes wide with fear. "You didn't," he said to the strange girl. "You set the clock *back*? You used it on them too? I thought we had to be careful. You told me to use it slowly, deliberately, or else we'd be pulled too far ahead."

"Mr. Lee?" Priyanka asked. "What is going on?"

"Oh, Albert," the girl said. "I'm sorry, but I couldn't resist. I was starting to show my age again, and I needed more time. We all need more time. Besides, I think I've almost deciphered the script that can move us *back*."

"Back?" Jill repeated, trying to follow this impossible conversation.

The girl turned to her. "We can't keep going forward. Not with the way things have turned out. I found the book all those years ago, figured out how to make it work, but only in one direction. Only forward. We *can't* keep going forward. Not anymore…"

"You shouldn't have kept them for so long," Mr. Lee said. "I'm principal now, and—"

"And you'll do what I say," growled the girl, who Jill realized was, impossibly, cranky old Mrs. Mosher. "Don't you forget, *I* was the one who kept you in on detention."

Jill scanned the room. There had to be a way out of this. She looked up at the clock, still ticking. An ancient artifact in this weirdly futuristic place.

And on the desk below it…Mrs. Mosher's old, leather-bound book.

She pushed past Mr. Lee and the girl, snatched the book off the desk and made a break for the doors.

"No!" Mrs. Mosher yelled. "Give that back! You have no idea how it works!"

"I don't care!" Jill cried, holding the book up in her hands. "You make one move toward me, and I'll…I'll tear it up!"

That stopped them both in their tracks.

"Come on, Priyanka," Jill said to her friend, who seemed frozen in fear. "We're getting out of here."

"Please don't damage the book," Mrs. Mosher said. "If you do, you'll ruin our chances of ever getting out of here."

Priyanka's eyes welled up with tears. "I want my mom," she choked out.

"Let's go find her then," Jill said. "C'mon!"

"Your mother is dead," Mrs. Mosher snapped. "In fact, everyone you know is dead. All *dead*!"

"We'll see about that," Jill said, taking Priyanka's hand and pushing open the door of the library.

"Yes, you'll see," Mrs. Mosher said, "and you'll be right back, I'm sure."

Jill and Priyanka went into the hallway. Only it wasn't anything like the hallway she had just been down. Sure, there were still photographs of graduating classes on the walls, only now there were hundreds of them. But the plastic frames were now rectangular pieces of metal, and the pictures

44

were holograms. Somehow the holograms looked like they were fading.

The hallway was lit with the same kind of window-like panels that Jill had seen in the library. They radiated light, but not all of them were working well. It was like the school had been thrust into a futuristic fantasy with high-tech improvements, but not everything was operational yet. And the closer Jill and Priyanka got to the front doors, the dirtier and dustier it got.

"Jill," Priyanka said, her voice almost a whisper.

"I know, I know," Jill said. "They've done something with time. We'll find someone who can fix it. We'll get back."

"No, that's not what I mean," Priyanka said. "Look at the classrooms!"

Jill stopped and turned. There were no students inside the rooms. No teachers either. The rooms were full of broken desks, burnt-out lights. Rats or some kind of small, rodent-like animals scurried. And the windows, those glowing replacement panels, were dirty and caked with dust. Jill noticed one that was broken.

She slowly walked toward it. Priyanka followed.

Light streamed through. Orange, murky light. Clutching the book to her chest, Jill stared out into the world beyond.

There had been a playground there long ago. But this was anything but. Concrete had crumbled, and the grass had burned to a crisp. An angry wind blew across the desolate wasteland. The sky was full of billowing clouds or smoke—Jill couldn't tell which. And everything boiled with an orange glow, although Jill could not actually see the sun through the thick haze.

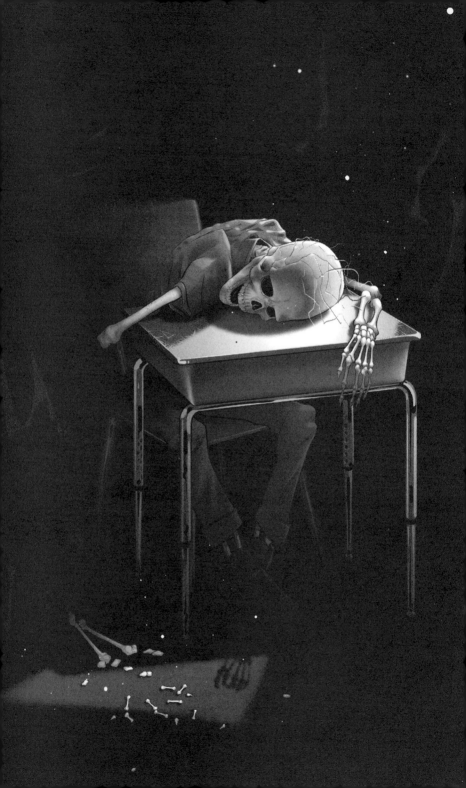

On the ceiling above them a screen crackled to life. Jill and Priyanka looked up and saw an image of Mrs. Mosher and Mr. Lee looking down at them. "Now you know," said Mrs. Mosher. "There's nothing left of them. It's just you and *us*."

Jill stepped back from the window. She opened the book and flipped through the pages until she found the diagram of the clock.

"What are you doing?" Mrs. Mosher asked frantically. Her face filled the entire screen above their heads, but Jill could still hear that clock in the library ticking away.

"No," Mrs. Mosher said. "Albert, go stop them! They don't understand. They'll only pull us further ahead!"

But Jill was focusing on the ticking clock. She didn't feel afraid anymore. Despite what Mrs. Mosher said, Jill *did* understand. The numbers and letters in the book made sense to her. She knew what to do.

"Stop them!" Mrs. Mosher cried. "They'll pull us *all* ahead!"

Jill could hear Mr. Lee's footsteps echoing down the empty hallway, but she honed in on the sound of the ticking clock.

Tick, tick, tick…

"You know what, Mrs. Mosher?" Jill said. "I don't think you've been behaving very nicely. In fact, I think it's time to put *you* in detention."

Jill held her gaze on the page. She focused on the sound of the clock and closed her eyes. "A nice, long detention."

Tick, tick, tick.

SEMI-DETACHED

Knock-knock.

Vijay pressed his ear up against the wall. He spread his hands out so the palms were flat against the cold, roughly painted surface. He took a deep breath and waited.

Knock-knock-knock! came the response.

Vijay smiled.

For years the neighbor in the townhouse to the left of Vijay's had been some old lady who was no fun. She just wanted peace and quiet, which was hard when you were Vijay and you wanted nothing more than to run up and down the stairs and scream a lot. But something happened to the old lady late one night. Vijay remembered the sirens and watching through his window as the ambulance attendants loaded her onto one of those stretchers. Vijay never heard the whole story, but it didn't matter, because soon enough Andrew had moved in next door.

Andrew was way more fun than that old lady, and, even better, he was Vijay's age. Plus, living in a row of town-houses meant that Vijay and Andrew were practically in the same house. There was just this thin wall separating their bedrooms. Vijay quickly discovered that if he knocked on the wall, Andrew could hear it pretty clearly on the other side.

The boys started banging back and forth, little rhythms at first but gradually getting more complicated, like they were playing drums to each other.

This annoyed the heck out of their parents and siblings, of course. Soon their parents cracked down on them. The boys were forbidden to communicate through the walls.

Despite this new law, Andrew and Vijay still made sure to sign off to one another before going to sleep. Each night just before Vijay was ready to turn out his lights, he would move over to the wall, press his ear against it and give it a couple of knocks. Not loud enough to wake anyone else up, mind you, but enough to let Andrew know he was off to sleep.

It was always Vijay who gave the final knock of the evening, and it was always Andrew who confirmed it with three knocks in a row.

That was their code. It was never spoken about. It was just something the boys secretly acknowledged as the way they said good night.

KNOCK-KNOCK-KNOCK!

Vijay nearly leaped from his bed. For a moment he thought there was an earthquake. It took him a few seconds to register that the floor wasn't shaking, the walls weren't caving in, it was just—

KNOCK-KNOCK-KNOCK.

Vijay stared at the wall.

"Andrew?" he whispered.

Crappers. Vijay turned to stare at his alarm clock on the bedside table. It was 1:13 a.m.

KNOCK-KNOCK-KNOCK.

Vijay heart pulsed hard with fear. It must be Andrew playing some kind of weird practical joke. Just Andrew on the other side of the wall, about to wake up their parents and get them both into trouble again.

KNOCK-KNOCK-KNOCK.

"All right, already!" Vijay snapped. He threw off the sheets and padded across the carpeted floor. The wall was smooth and thick and draped with the kinds of dark shadows that only the middle of the night can bring forth.

Vijay gave the wall a few well-placed knocks. "Now cut it out and let me sleep," he said in what he hoped was not such a loud voice that it would wake the rest of his family.

Satisfied that Andrew had given up on his joke, Vijay turned and trudged back to bed. He closed his eyes and after a few moments drifted back into a deep slumber.

The next morning on the way to school, Vijay waited until he and Andrew were alone to broach the subject. "*You* were up late," he said, stopping on the sidewalk.

Andrew blinked. "Was I?"

"Like, one in the morning isn't late?"

"What are you talking about, Vijay?"

"Come on. You know what I mean. The knocking."

"On the walls?"

"It wasn't coming from the ceiling."

"Why would I be knocking on the walls at one in the morning?"

"I don't know, you tell me."

"Dude, I was asleep." Andrew thought for a second. "Although I have…well…sleepwalked in the past."

"There you go," Vijay said. "That explains it."

"You think I sleepwalked and sleep-knocked?"

"You were doing something," Vijay said. "Our rooms are right next to each other. Whatever you were up to, you were banging pretty loudly."

In silence the boys began to walk again. Vijay was going over the events of the previous night in his head and assumed that Andrew was doing the same.

This time it was Andrew who stopped. "But I didn't wake anyone else up, did I?" he asked.

"You were pretty loud, man. Like, *loud*."

Three nights later it happened again.

Vijay had almost forgotten about the first incident. Three days was just about enough time to clear most things from his head. But sure enough, sometime in the quiet hours of the night, when he was in the middle of a dream, an almost deafening knock jolted Vijay awake.

Heart in his throat, Vijay stared at the wall opposite his bed.

In the near darkness of the room, the wall seemed to absorb the shadows of everything else around it. It stood silently, as walls do, but somehow *this* wall seemed different from the other three encircling him. Closer, perhaps? *Thicker? Angrier?* Vijay struggled to determine how the wall had changed and found that he did not want to stare at it any longer. He averted his gaze to the one source of light in the room, his alarm clock.

It read 1:13. The red digits of the clock glowed.

Vijay blinked, thinking this was some weird kind of déjà vu. One thirteen? That was when he'd woken up the other night, only...

He blinked again.

KNOCK-KNOCK!

The sound was so loud that Vijay felt it jiggle his bones. He screamed—or tried to. His mouth was open, but no sound came out.

The knocking continued, more softly now. There were fast knocks, then pauses between the knocks. Vijay sat in his bed, covers pulled up to his neck, trying to figure out what Andrew was doing.

For somebody supposedly sleepwalking, the guy certainly seemed wide awake.

"Andrew," Vijay said to himself. "It's only Andrew. Only Andrew in his sleep." He repeated this a few more times until he felt brave enough to push back the covers, slide out of bed and slowly, gingerly, pace over to the wall.

The knocking continued. At first it seemed to be coming from one place on the wall, right where Andrew often knocked. But as Vijay tried to nail down the source, it moved. First alongside the wall, as if Andrew were pacing the room.

And then up.

As if Andrew had stepped onto a chair.

Then the knocking moved too far up, too high, for it to be coming from Andrew on a chair.

And it kept moving.

Vijay stood back from the wall, shaking his head. It's got to be some kind of prank, he thought. That must be it. Andrew had orchestrated this event to occur at precisely the same time as before, using a strange series of knocks to give him a good, solid scare.

Cripes, it was working!

It was harder to tell which knocking was louder—Andrew's hand against the wall or the pounding heart in Vijay's chest.

But it was just Andrew up to some stupid trick, nothing to be afraid of. Vijay took a deep breath, swallowed and went back to the wall.

He pressed his hands against it, took a deep breath and then reached back with his hand to give the wall a good, solid knock.

BAM!

And on cue the knocking stopped.

Vijay nodded. He let out a shaky breath and smiled. *That'll teach him.*

KNOCK-KNOCK-KNOCK!

The sound was so intense, it nearly threw Vijay off his feet.

And somehow it seemed to be coming from *inside* the wall.

Vijay dashed back to his bed, pulled the covers tightly around him and lay there shivering until some time later—much later—he finally fell asleep.

"What the heck, dude? You scared the living crap out of me!"

And it showed. Vijay's skin was pale, and there were dark circles under his eyes. This time, though, they were from staying up past midnight playing video games.

Andrew shook his head. "I was sleepwalking again?"

"Come on. That wasn't sleepwalking or sleep-knocking."

The boys were walking to school again, only today Vijay hung back from Andrew, still a bit miffed. How much sleep had he lost on account of Andrew and his bad joke?

"Vijay, it wasn't me. At least, not *awake* me."

Vijay shrugged. Andrew could be telling the truth. "Whatever you want to call it. It was *weird*."

"I bet," Andrew said. "But honestly, I had no idea I was doing it. So I scared the crap out of you, did I?"

"You want to check my underwear for stains?" Vijay asked. "Be my guest. But you were knocking all over the place. Up and down. Soft and loud. Like, really loud! And the knocks had all kinds of pauses and breaks."

"Between the knocks?" Andrew said.

Vijay nodded. "Yeah, short and long. Super annoying."

Andrew frowned. "Pauses and breaks," he said again. "Like I was knocking in code or something?"

The boys stopped and stared at one another.

"Morse code is a series of long and short pauses between signals," Andrew said. "Remember me telling you about that cool book I read?"

"That must be what you were doing. Sending me messages. Right?"

Andrew turned away. "Except I don't know Morse code."

"You must have picked it up somewhere. Maybe from that book."

"Yeah, but I don't remember the code itself. I just read about it."

"That must be it though. Who knows *what* kinds of things your brain does when you fall asleep."

"I don't think so, Vijay."

But Vijay was convinced. "That's the only explanation I can think of. Your *sleep* brain, right? It gets you knocking Morse code and wakes you up at precisely one thirteen in the morning."

"I guess…" said Andrew, clearly not convinced.

"Well, you tell that sleep brain of yours to cut it out. I really need to get some sleep."

Andrew did cut it out. For a little bit, at any rate. But a few days later, the knocks came back. Just as before, at 1:13 a.m., and also just as before, in a series of knocks that Vijay had to admit sounded like some kind of signal. Some knocks had longer breaks between them, while others were much shorter.

This time Vijay was ready.

He fumbled on his bedside table for his phone, switched it on and found the app that activated the audio recorder. Then he pointed it at the wall and waited.

The boys didn't have any time to decode the message while they were at school the next day. But after dinner Andrew came over to Vijay's house for a sleepover. They holed themselves up in Vijay's room, got distracted playing video games for a while, but eventually found a Morse decoder online and got to work.

Andrew was a whiz with letters, so he was in charge of deciphering the code.

"Okay, play it again. More slowly this time," he said.

Vijay hit the Play button. Andrew closed his eyes for a moment, straining to hear, and then motioned for Vijay to stop the recording. He eyed the Morse decoder and scribbled down some of the letters. "S-T-O-P-K-N-O-C-K-I-N-G."

"Stop *knocking*?" Vijay repeated. "Why would you tell me to stop knocking? It was *you* knocking in the first place."

Andrew shrugged. "Turns out I'm really good at this Morse code stuff though."

Vijay played the next part of the message, and Andrew quickly deciphered it.

"YOU-ARE-WAKING-ME-UP."

Vijay shook his head. "Again, it was you doing the knocking, man."

Andrew looked from the recorder and the decoding information over to the wall. He stared at it for another moment. "Honestly, I have no memory of getting up and knocking."

"But you said you sleepwalk."

"Yeah, a few times, when I was younger. But I haven't done that for *years*. I asked my mom about it too. She didn't notice me getting up or anything. When I was a kid, I'd be walking all over the house. I never did something like going to the wall and banging my fist against it."

"Come on. Let's do the rest of the message."

Andrew frowned. He kept frowning as he deciphered the next part of the message.

"ALL DAY YOU MAKE NOISE. SO MUCH NOISE AND SO MUCH KNOCKING. FOR YEARS AND YEARS."

He turned to Vijay. "I really don't like this. It's freaking me out a bit, dude."

"Hang on," Vijay said. "There's one last bit." He played the last of the recording, and Andrew scribbled the letters onto the paper. He looked at what he'd written, and his face went white.

"What? What is it?" Vijay asked, but Andrew didn't respond. Vijay moved over to the edge of the bed where Andrew was sitting and pulled the paper out of his hands.

KNOCK ONE MORE TIME AND I WILL STOP YOU FOR GOOD.

Vijay blinked. He looked at Andrew, but Andrew was staring at the wall.

Then Vijay let out a long, shaky sigh. His face broke into a big, broad grin. "Oh, you are hilarious, man!" He clapped Andrew on the back. "Hilarious! You really stretched this joke out. Good idea, getting me to believe you actually could decode Morse code. Getting me to think that maybe it was a ghost or something…"

Vijay got up and went over to the wall.

Andrew shook his head. "Vijay, no. I don't think that's a good idea."

"Oh, you don't, do you?"

Andrew stood up. "I mean it. Move away from the wall."

"What? This wall? This one right *here*?!" As he said the words, Vijay gave the wall a good, hard slap with the palm of his hand.

"Vijay, aren't you listening? I'm not making this up! The messages are real. It's *all* real!"

Vijay shook his head. "Come on, man. The only thing going on around here that's real is this flipping wall!"

And he turned away from Andrew, balled his hands into fists and started hammering all over the wall. "Best! Joke! Ever!"

He hammered for a good thirty seconds, until his fists were hurting. Then he just stood there, breathing heavily.

That's when he noticed something curious. At first he thought he'd left handprints on the wall from knocking on it so hard.

But the handprints weren't his. They were bigger. And the palms faced out.

Vijay squinted, backing away slightly. "What the—?"

Then the handprints moved.

They followed Vijay, and then they extended out of the wall itself, so quickly that Vijay didn't have a chance to back away farther. The hands pushed right through the wall, and Vijay could see ghostly white arms reaching for him. They grabbed him by his collar and lifted him up off the floor.

Vijay tried to scream, but nothing came out. His feet were now a foot or so off the floor, and he was choking!

Andrew jumped off the bed and raced over to help Vijay, to pull him down, but the arms were too strong. Then suddenly Vijay dropped back down, not because Andrew had tried harder, but because one of the hands had let go.

The free hand reached out and grabbed Andrew by the collar too.

Andrew screamed.

The hands were cold and rough. They were covered with plaster and bits of brick and insulation. The grit from the hands got into the boys' skin, and it burned.

Vijay finally found his voice and screamed too. Because he could see the wall around the hands starting to crack and break. Fissures appeared. The arms were pulling him and Andrew closer, toward the giant crack in the wall. In the dark of the crack, Vijay could see a face.

Maybe just part of a face—

An angry face—

A face kind of like that old lady's face, the lady who had lived next door before—

Vijay turned away from the face in terror. His eyes fell on his clock. It was flashing.

1:13 a.m.

COLOR SCHEME

Diego dabbed the brush into the paint. He raised it to his face and stared at the jellylike glob. Something about it didn't smell quite right. It was like the paint had come from a bottle as old as time itself.

Also, the color was off. It was supposed to be blue, but this shade was only slightly so. Diego tried to figure out what colors might have been mixed to create this hue, but kept coming back to what colors it *wasn't*: not purple, not indigo. It just wasn't a color that fit into the spectrum he had grown up with.

Diego shrugged and ran the paintbrush across the clean white page, smearing the not-quite-blue in a wobbly line.

He lifted the brush and stared at the gash of color. Not only did this sample of paint smell and look different, but it also didn't *feel* quite like the paints he'd used in the past. Not that he painted often.

Most of his art teachers had stuck to pastels and pencil crayons, with maybe a little bit of collage thrown in to mix things up a bit. But painting? Forget it. It was messy. It meant laying dropsheets over desks, drying tables and rinsing thirty brushes. Too much setup and cleanup.

But the new art teacher wasn't bothered about students making a mess.

Mr. Cook had arrived at Diego's school only a few weeks earlier, when Mrs. Massey had left to have a baby. Everyone loved Mrs. Massey. She always spoke quietly and radiated a kind of calm that made Diego feel calm too.

Mr. Cook, on the other hand, buzzed around like a stick insect that had downed a case of energy drinks. From the first day, he was passionate about getting the students to experiment with all kinds of art forms: papier-mâché, clay sculpture and now painting.

Diego turned his attention away from the gelatinous splotch on his paintbrush to the slightly manic teacher whirling about the classroom. With his wild gray hair bouncing, Mr. Cook handed out papers and palettes with the kind of glee you'd expect of a kid on Halloween.

Most of the students had the same kind of bewildered looks on their faces as Diego had.

"What do you want us to paint?" Lexi asked, twirling her brush in the air. "You didn't exactly give us a lesson. Also, what happens if we get paint on our clothes? Is it going to come out in the wash? I just got this shirt."

"Yes, yes, you'll want to mix the colors," Mr. Cook said, his eyes not quite meeting the students, his answers not quite meeting the questions.

He floated by Diego's desk and squirted another glob of paint on Diego's palette from a tube in his jittery hands. Now added to the not-quite-blue and definitely-only-somewhat-red was an uncertain shade of...

"Is that meant to be green?" Lexi asked as Mr. Cook squirted a blob on her palette with such force that flecks of it spattered onto her clothes.

Mr. Cook flashed a massive grin. "You should experiment with the colors and find out!"

Diego watched as the teacher darted from desk to desk, squirting color like he was Santa Claus delivering presents. There didn't seem to be any method to his madness. He flitted about the classroom randomly. In fact, Diego wasn't sure if everyone in the room ever got the materials they needed.

At some point Mr. Cook decided his work was finished. "If you'll excuse me for a moment," he said and then slipped out the door.

Diego's classmates took advantage of a few minutes of freedom. Marcus, for instance, was flicking paint across the room. Spatters were getting all over the floor, the desks and the back of Lexi's shirt.

Diego shifted his gaze to Mr. Cook's desk. It was its usual mess of scattered papers and assignments, almost all of them unmarked or graded. It looked less like the workspace of a teacher and more like the contents of a recycling bin.

But what caught Diego's eye was the desk drawer that had been pulled open.

More papers were spilling out of it. Diego noticed that some of these papers were covered in Mr. Cook's almost unintelligible scrawl. They didn't look like typical notes. There were numbers and symbols mixed in.

Equations.

In fact, Diego could see that most of the scraps of paper were covered in this scrawl. It looked like the kind of crazy calculations and equations you'd see on blackboards in old science fiction movies, the ones where scientists broke the very laws of nature itself.

From behind came a loud crash. Marcus, no doubt. Why not? Mr. Cook had left the room. He should have known that this was not the kind of class a teacher could take their eyes off for even a second without some kind of catastrophe going down.

Diego stiffened.

Mr. Cook *hadn't* taken his eyes off the classroom.

There he was on the other side of the closed door, staring in through the glass window, wearing a pair of sunglasses.

No, not sunglasses, *goggles*. Dark goggles strapped around his head with an elastic. They looked weird, and so did Mr. Cook, standing there looking in and not entering.

Diego moved away from the desk, ignoring the splashes he heard elsewhere in the room. There were other noises too— students getting into some kind of mischief. But what was the deal with Mr. Cook and those goggles?

TALES FROM THE FRINGES OF FEAR

Diego positioned himself at the door so that he was almost eye to eye with his teacher. "Mr. Cook?" he asked.

All Mr. Cook did was smile.

Man, that guy was weird.

Diego reached out to open the door. It was locked.

He tried the handle again and then turned the little lock mechanism. It wouldn't move because Mr. Cook had his key in the lock and was holding it in place.

A loud squelch sounded behind him, then a heavy splash, like someone had deliberately jammed their foot into the bucket of water used for rinsing the paintbrushes.

Diego turned.

Someone *had* dumped the bucket. There was a pool of liquid spreading across the floor.

And there was a small heap of clothing. Boys' clothing. Marcus's clothing, to be exact. Diego could tell from the jeans and the T-shirt with the image of a great white shark emblazoned on it.

But no Marcus.

A small crowd had begun to gather around the puddle. The looks on their faces quickly went from disbelief to fear.

Diego let go of the door handle and edged toward the puddle.

He heard a scream and whirled around just as the scream shifted into a gurgle. From the corner of his eye he caught sight of something where Lexi had been sitting a few moments earlier. There was a blur of motion, a loud splash and the *slap* of wet clothing hitting the tiled floor.

Lexi's clothes.

A thick, gelatinous puddle spread menacingly around them.

Diego backed away.

"Lexi?" he called. She did not reply.

Then more cries that became gurgles. Diego turned and saw something he could not make sense of.

Aria had been a few paces away from Lexi. She'd been right there, Diego had seen her with his own eyes, and then she was *not*.

It took less than a second. Her whole body changed, shifted, *melted*.

Yes, melted.

And for the tiniest moment there was an aqueous substance that held Aria's form. Then gravity took over, and her clothes crumpled to the floor. No blood. No bones. No organs to spatter across the tile. Just a thick, oozing, clear liquid.

There was another scream, and it took Diego a second to realize it was coming from him.

Splash!

One moment Diego was looking at Natalie Kaganski holding her paintbrush, staring down at her desk, and the next moment...she was gone, just like Aria. Just like Lexi. And Mark.

Splash! Splash!

All around Diego, kids were dropping and turning into puddles. He took a step and slipped, his feet suddenly above his head.

Next thing he knew, he was flat on his back with oozing puddle gunk all over him. It was in his hair, it was on his back, and it was making his clothes cling to his skin.

He screamed again and scrambled to his feet—or tried to. It was like trying to stand up on jello.

He wiped his hands clean on the only dry bit left on his shirt, then clung to the edge of a chair to pull himself up. It took a while. That's when Diego realized two things. First, he was the only student left in the room who was not a puddle of goo, and second, Mr. Cook had unlocked the door and reentered the room.

"Last one standing," Mr. Cook said. He sounded slightly dissatisfied. "I thought it might be Marcus."

"What have you done?" Diego cried.

The thick liquid was pooling around Diego's ankles now, ebbing and flowing like an ocean tide. He swore he could even hear an anguished sigh bubbling up out of the substance.

He had to think. There must be a way to get past Mr. Cook, get out of the room, warn the others.

Think. The teacher still had those ridiculous goggles on. Why?

"The experiment was a success," Mr. Cook said.

"Experiment? You've murdered them!"

Mr. Cook made a face and gave a dismissive wave. "Don't be obtuse. They don't hire murderers to teach art. What do you take me for?"

Diego gripped the chair so tightly that his knuckles nearly burst through the skin. He pivoted and kept his eyes firmly fixed on Mr. Cook. "What experiment are you talking about?"

The teacher went to his desk and pulled out some of the papers Diego had spotted there. "You saw my rough notes. I may have left the room, but I've been watching you the whole time."

"The equations," Diego said.

"They weren't hiring chemistry teachers, but I figured a homeroom class with some art-prep periods would suffice. This is really just the first stage of the plan, at any rate."

Keep him talking, Diego thought, eyes locked on his teacher. Keep him confident. Look for your moment. He's away from the door, and if you can manage to leap past that puddle, you can probably get out into the hallway, warn someone—

"You're thinking about escaping," Mr. Cook said. He broke Diego's gaze and nodded to the room. "That's what I'd do, if I were you. I'm far enough away that I'm unlikely to stop you. So by all means, give it your best try."

Diego's stomach did a nosedive. "What's the catch?"

"You think I'm going to chase you through that primordial slime? For starters, it's disgusting, and besides, I need to keep the sample *pure*."

Pure. The thought of all his classmates on the floor made Diego feel sick.

He opened his mouth, but instead of unleashing his lunch, he let out a slow, deliberate breath. The door was less than fifteen feet away.

He broke Mr. Cook's icy stare and searched for the right path. The pool of ooze was still spreading, but if he bolted, he could jump, grab the edge of the next desk to propel himself, and then he'd be out of it, out the door and into the—

Paint.

Diego's gaze fell short of the door. The paint had caught his eye.

The colors had mixed together on the paper. It was Natalie's paper, the one she'd been staring at, right before she'd...

The colors.

Diego had never seen anything quite like it before. Sure, that blue he'd smeared across his page hadn't seemed right, but with a little bit of the not-so-green and the definitely-not-purple, why, it was a different sight altogether. The combination was mesmerizing. Hypnotic. No colors had ever looked like the ones on Natalie's abandoned paper. They seemed to pulse and throb with life. It was almost as if a rift had opened up there on the page, with the colors beckoning him.

"That's right," Mr. Cook's voice soothed. "You're seeing it now. And once you do, you can't unsee it. Your eyes need to take it all in. And not just your eyes. There's the rest of you too!"

Diego's heart throbbed in his chest. He knew it was dangerous. That he should look away.

Only he couldn't. The colors were calling out to him. Although Diego registered fear, another part of his brain—presumably the part connected to his ocular nerve—resisted.

"It's pulling you closer," Mr. Cook's voice urged, not that Diego had the willpower to tear his gaze away from the paper. "Muscle, organs, molecules. It's drawing you in, taking you back. Way back. Taking your body to a time that existed long before evolution spun us out into these ungainly, solid forms."

What was it Mr. Cook had called the ooze? *Primordial slime?*

Diego made one last-ditch effort to look away, to turn his neck or close his eyelids, but his body resisted. The painted colors now filled up his entire field of vision. They were coursing through his body, until he felt his muscles shimmer, his bones melt—

Splash!

But it wasn't the end. Not of his mind anyway.

His body? Unclear.

Diego could feel *something*, but it wasn't like anything his corporeal body had registered before. What was left of his mind wanted to scream, but there were no lungs to draw air from, no mouth to open. He wanted to get up and run, but there were no arms to push himself off the ground with, no muscles or bones to make any kind of movement.

He undulated on the cold floor tiles, sensing light above him, sensing vibrations in the air around him.

If he thought long enough about it, if Diego flexed the part of his mind that was still his own, he knew that he was oozing to the left. Then to the right. He could control it if he wanted to—

Hey! Get out of my space!

It was not a voice, but a presence nonetheless. He sensed it pushing around him, pooling at his left side, dividing him down the middle so that he was in two parts.

The lower part drifted one way into the ooze, the upper part in the opposite direction.

I'm split! Diego was worried.

Yeah, yeah. We're all split.

That voice seemed familiar. Diego concentrated hard, trying to remember who it belonged to…

Marcus? Is that you?

It was *me,* the other presence somehow articulated. *But there* is *no me anymore. There is no you anymore.*

That can't be, Diego thought, more terrified than ever. The fear made him lengthen and ooze in several directions at once. He suddenly found himself in a number of other pools, those of his liquefied peers.

Gross! came another thought wave. That had to be Lexi. *Get out of here, you jerk! Stop freaking out and mixing us together! Do you have any idea how long it's going to take for us to get back to the way we were?*

There's no going back. Diego knew this blob was Natalie.

Diego was panicking. There had to be some way out of this mess. Literally, it was a mess. He, Marcus, Lexi—the whole darn class was all mixed together in a slop on the floor.

And then came the shadow.

He sensed it above him, not quite seeing it but aware of the light being blotted out by a large object.

Mr. Cook?

No, not him. Diego rippled under the weight of heavy footsteps approaching. The vibrations were too strong. Not Mr. Cook. Boots too heavy. They could only belong to—

Something solid slammed against the floor and into Diego's very substance.

What is it? a disembodied voice called out beside him.

Mop! Diego cried. *Mr. Peary, the caretaker!*

And then he was entwined in the fibers of the mop. The human Diego would have let out a piercing scream, but there were no screams to be made in this new state. The mop head slid against the floor, and the last remaining bit of the pool that was entirely Diego was now thoroughly mixed with the parts of his former classmates.

He felt parts of himself lifting away from the floor, half-absorbed by the mop and half-dripping in little splatters everywhere. Mr. Peary squeezed the mop head and splashed it back into the dirty bucket. This kind of torture would have caused Diego great pain if he had still had the nerve endings to feel such things.

Panic, on the other hand, continued to pulse through him.

"I know you can understand me," a voice called from the darkness. Not that Diego registered it as a voice in the way that his human self could. Still, the message was being communicated.

"I must apologize for the messy means of collecting you, but I had to make it look like an accident, hence the caretaker and his bucket. It's not as if the school would allow me to take specimens in the conventional way."

Parts of Diego were now moving in various directions across a big, wide surface. Other bits of his aqueous self were on something dark and bristly. A paintbrush?

"But the experiment was a success," Mr. Cook continued. "You've reverted to a form of life that predated organisms in the way that we've come to know them. A living, thinking biofilm. Isn't that fascinating? And because you've all been mixed together, you're going to have to live together that way. No fighting. No wars. You will be at peace."

Diego was aware of his classmates around him. He could sense their minds, spinning in various directions, trying to take in their new world. If he concentrated hard enough, he could feel the fibers of the canvas holding him—and the others—in place.

A painting. But of what?

"For goodness' sake, will you take off those ridiculous goggles?" Diego's father snapped at the batty-looking teacher. There had to be at least fifty parents gathered in the entryway of the school. The flashing lights of a small squadron of police cars outside cast the room in an alternating glow of blue and red.

"Where is the principal?" another mother asked, her voice choked with fear.

"Please, please," the tall man with the wild gray hair said, motioning them to calm down. "I've already arranged to solve this problem once and for all."

"Solve this problem? What on earth are you talking about?" Diego's father growled. "Our children are *missing*. The whole class! You're their teacher. You should know something. Where did they all go?"

But Mr. Cook had turned away from them. He was busy adjusting the last painting on the wall.

"Stop fussing with those paintings!" Diego's father yelled. "The police are outside. We demand answers!"

But Mr. Cook merely motioned to the paintings on the wall. The paint still looked wet. There were lots of different images, but there were words overlaid on them too. Words like *LOOK HERE* and *SEE ME*.

Diego's father found himself studying the paintings more carefully. Suddenly the anger in him was replaced with another feeling altogether.

The others parents noticed the art on the walls too.

"What beautiful colors," said Diego's mother, reaching out to touch one of the paintings. "I've never seen anything quite like it before."

THE WAY OF THE GOLEM

I stared at the word in the ancient script. The letters were Hebrew, which should have been easy enough to translate, but it's not like I paid *actual* attention in Hebrew school.

"The word is *emet*," Seth said, shaking his head. I must have been giving him a serious blank look. "Truth," he said again, like he was speaking to a small child.

"Word up," I said, and tried to fist-bump him.

"No. The first, middle and last letter of the Hebrew alphabet mean 'emet,' or 'truth.'"

"Gotcha." I nodded, although I still didn't understand what Seth was getting at.

Seth held the script closer to me and jabbed a finger at the letters. "You write *that* word down on whatever you make from the clay. You've got to use those three exact Hebrew letters, in that order, or it won't work."

"Sure thing," I said again. It's not like I truly believed anything Seth was saying. But there was this tiny part of my mind that wondered...*what if?*

"I've done the translation."

Seth pulled a folded piece of paper from his pocket and handed it to me. I opened it up and saw a bunch of nonsensical English words, phonetically translated from Hebrew, I guessed. "So you read this incantation," he continued, "and the clay will come *to life*."

The way he said it, I got this image of the Frankenstein monster getting hit with a bolt of lightning. I had seen that old black-and-white movie that came on TV every Halloween. "Uh, okay," I said.

Seth fixed me with the kind of stare that suggested just how big an idiot he thought I was. "We are all but clay in the hands of our maker," he said. "That is the way of the golem."

"The golem?" I asked, ignoring the fact that Seth was acting, like, super weird.

"A being of clay, brought to life with the right words. Justin, I already *told* you this. Are you even listening to me?"

I nodded blankly. "Sure thing, Seth."

He waved me off. "Trust me, it'll work."

I had known Seth since we were little. He was the rabbi's son, and he was not cool. It wasn't like he made much of an effort to try to fit in. He was always tucked away in a corner of the room in whatever free time we had, drawing and sketching. He kept a spare pencil behind his ear at all times, in case he found something to draw.

But at least I talked to him. The other guys in our class were pretty big jerks when it came to Seth. They were the ones who teased him for being a rabbi's son and razzed him about never being able to do anything fun on a Saturday, like play hockey, or stay out late on a Friday night. They were the ones who threw spitballs, who rubbed bacon grease onto his clothes, who called him names. Not me.

Not *always*.

So, yeah, I guess Seth and I were friends. Oh, it's not like we were inseparable besties. I mean, I saw him at school but steered clear of him when the other guys were giving him a hard time. I mean, why make my life difficult? But sometimes, when we carpooled to after-school Hebrew lessons at the synagogue, Seth would draw his pictures for me. We had an understanding.

Which is why I guess he told me about the mystical book in the first place.

It all started one day before our after-school Hebrew lessons. Seth had told me about this old book of mystical spells that his dad kept at the synagogue, how he'd overheard him talking about it with one of his colleagues. The colleague had wanted the book back, but Seth's father wouldn't let him have it. They'd gotten into an argument. Seth had heard the man say that the book had a series of incantations that could bring a creature made out of clay to life. It ended with Rabbi Silverstein insisting the man leave the synagogue at once.

Seth said he wanted me to come help him find the incantations from that book.

Even if the incantations turned out to be a load of baloney, it was kind of cool to sneak into the back library of the synagogue. I'd only ever seen the main prayer hall and the classrooms where we did our Hebrew lessons.

The back library was really creepy, but I *loved* hanging out in creepy places. It was a cobwebby backroom without windows, lit only by a single hanging bulb. It had probably been a closet at one point or a place to put important stuff. Old Torah scrolls in need of repair were leaning against the walls. The shelves were lined with old, dusty books.

The one Seth had pulled off the shelf certainly looked old, even older than the synagogue. The book had thick, yellowed pages, and the wobbly Hebrew lettering on its surface felt like it had crawled in from a time of myths and legends.

Even Seth seemed spooked as he leafed through the pages. He kept looking over his shoulder, clearly afraid of us getting caught back there.

Then he reached into a pocket, pulled out his cell phone and started taking pictures of some of the pages.

"There's no way I can read that," I told him.

"But I can," Seth said. "I'll find a way to translate it for you, and we can try out some of these spells."

"Sure thing," I said, really not believing him at the time.

I wasn't sure I believed him even now, but it was worth seeing where this was all going.

Seth wasn't too specific about the actual clay you needed to use. I had managed to swipe a small pack of modeling clay from my teacher's supply cupboard. It wasn't much, but it would do. I got right to work on it after school, when I was meant to be doing homework. It didn't take me too long to push and pull the clay into the approximate shape of a person, although it was pretty rough. My sculpture had a pair of thick, stubby legs, two appendages for arms, and a sort of head. Sculpture wasn't really my area of expertise.

Referring to the note Seth had given me, I took a sharpened pencil and carved the three letters onto the head of the little clay man, read the words off the paper and waited.

Nothing happened.

I waited some more.

The clay man stood there, completely inert.

"Great." I scowled. Seth had played a great trick on me. When I got to school the next day, I'd be sure to—

The clay head turned in my direction.

Not much. Not enough to make me scream, but enough to stop me in mid-thought. Enough to stop me from taking in my next breath.

The clay man slowly lifted its "arm" and stared at it, like it was wondering what the heck it was. It lifted a foot, wiggled it in the air and planted it down again. It lifted the other foot before shifting its weight from side to side. It stopped, then looked in my direction, which was totally creepy, especially since it had no eyes or face.

It looked like it was waiting for me to say something.

At this point, I realized how dry my throat had become. I coughed, swallowed and looked around the room. It was about as messy as they come. All my clothes were strewn about the floor as if some sort of laundry tornado had landed here. "Pick up my clothes," I said meekly. "And pile them up in the corner?" I didn't mean for it to come out as a question.

The clay man—I guessed this was what Seth meant by a golem—gave me a slight nod of understanding and then went to work.

I sat there, my mouth hanging open, watching the little man grab my clothes, piece by piece, and drag them across the floor to the corner, just as I'd asked.

When all the clothes were piled, it waddled back over to me and stood there, waiting for my next command.

"Uhhh…" I started.

A loud knock at the door startled me.

"Justin!" It was my mom. "Dinner's ready in five!"

"Coming!" I called, not taking my eyes off the golem for a second.

The little creature stood in place. "Go under the bed," I told it. "Stay there until I tell you to come out."

A moment passed. The golem didn't nod or anything, but I had the feeling that some kind of understanding had passed between us. The clay creature waddled over to my bed and slid into the space between my bed and the floor.

I stood there, staring.

I never told the golem to come *out* from under my bed. To be honest, the thing freaked me out. I spent half the night leaning over with my flashlight and taking peeks at it. It stayed as still as the statue I'd initially formed from the clay. That made it even more unsettling.

Seth showed up late for school the next day. I could only assume he had stayed up all night, like I had, tinkering with clay. He looked tired enough. I didn't have time to talk to him until lunch. As usual he was over in a corner, away from the rest of us, his head in a book. I got his attention the way I always did—I went up really close, sat down beside him and poked him in the ribs.

"Hey, quit it!" Seth yelled.

"Sorry, dude," I said. "But I need to know something about…" I looked around the room and then leaned in closer. "About those instructions you gave me," I whispered.

Seth put the book down. "It worked, didn't it?"

I nodded.

"I thought so," he said. "So what did you make it do?"

"Pick up my clothes." It sounded so lame now.

Seth laughed. "Well, I guess that's a start."

"One question," I said.

"What's that?"

"How do you make the golem…you know…*stop*?" I tried to explain what I meant. "Like, being a golem." I didn't think I would ever get a good night's sleep with that thing under my bed.

Seth smiled. "All in due time, Justin. First I want to show you something."

Seth said to meet him after school at the ravine near the subdivision we both lived in. It seemed like a weird spot, but Seth insisted we rendezvous there or there'd be no magical formula.

I followed him down a winding path into the forest until we reached a totally secluded spot. We were surrouded by thick green trees that blocked out much of the light from the sun. "Exactly why are we meeting here?" I asked. "It looks like a crime scene or something."

Seth shook his head. "Guess again."

"C'mon, Seth," I said. "You said you were going to tell me how to get rid of that golem under my bed."

"And I will." He smiled mysteriously.

I suddenly realized that the previous night was probably not the first time Seth had tried the incantation.

"Seth, how long have you been making your own golems?"

He nodded. "Yes, I admit, I've made golems before," he said. "Little ones at first, probably like the one you created last night."

I nodded, waiting for him to explain.

"But *small* is *boring*." Seth motioned at the ravine. "So I dug up some clay from this creek and started making them larger. Then I made them fight one another here. But that got boring too. It's kind of like playing chess against yourself. You can do it, but it's more fun with an opponent. So I figured I'd need someone to do battle with." Seth stared at me. It was a little creepy.

"You want a duel of *golems*?" I asked.

Seth smiled. "Now that you know the incantations, we can bring our own golems to life and have them fight each other. What do you say to that?"

I looked around the quiet ravine. "I don't know…"

"Come on," Seth said, putting his hand on my shoulder. "It'll be way better than any video game."

Seth was right.

We went over to the creek bed and began scooping the muddy clay. In no time we'd each constructed a clay figure roughly the size of a large snowman. With Seth directing, we spoke the incantations and brought the golems to life. With heavy movements, they began to move and twist their misshapen limbs and then lumber about the base of the ravine. I marched my golem to the other side of the shallow creek bed, and then we had the two monsters come at each other and duke it out in the mud.

All I had to do was think about how I wanted the golem to move, and it did what my mind pictured. If I thought about ducking, the golem ducked. If I thought about grabbing hold of Seth's creature, my golem managed to grab hold of his and flip it over. That is, unless Seth focused his thoughts on a better defensive move and pinned my golem to the muddy earth instead.

We went at it with the two golems for a couple of hours, until the sun was starting to set.

I had told my mom I was going to be out late, but not *this* late. My brain was tired. It was hard work doing all that concentrating. "Hey, Seth, can you show me how to switch these guys off now?"

Seth nodded. He handed me another piece of paper. "Try saying this," he said.

I went over to my golem and read the words on the paper. The creature looked at me for a moment, seeming a bit off-balance, and then went completely still. I tapped it with my finger. The golem did not react. My finger made a slight dent in the wet clay.

Seth was saying something to his golem too. Only it didn't sound quite like what I had said to mine. I watched as he leaned in close to his creature and wiped something off its forehead. He wiped the wet clay against his pants and then did the same to my golem.

"What are you doing?" I asked.

"Nothing important," Seth said, but it looked as if he'd smeared out part of the writing we'd put on the foreheads of our golems. Then he came up to me, really close this time. There was a new gleam in his eyes. "So you want to do something totally crazy?"

"What do you mean?"

"I tried out something new the other day. Something I'd never done with the golems before."

"Like what?"

"I got *inside* one of them."

I narrowed my eyes. "What are you talking about?"

"I went back to that book from the synagogue when my dad wasn't looking. Did a little exploring. Did you know there are incantations that actually allow you to shift right into the golem? So you can *wear* it, like a suit?"

He dug into his pocket and pulled out a slip of paper. Written on it was another series of phonetic syllables.

I hesitated.

"We'll do it together," he said. "We can come back late tonight, when no one's around."

"You're talking about going inside the clay?" I shook my head. "Wouldn't you suffocate?"

Seth shook his head. "The spell ensures you can still breathe, talk and keep control of the golem."

Then he pointed across the creek. I hadn't noticed it before, but several trees looked as if they'd been snapped in half by something big and powerful.

"*You* did that?"

"The golem did. I just controlled it."

"It knocked over the trees?"

"I'll show you how, if you want."

I nodded. It *was* pretty cool.

"It'll have to be later though," Seth said. "When there's no chance of us being seen."

He extended the paper toward me. I stared at it for a moment or two. The words had power, that much I knew. And to be honest, that power had felt really good when we were using our minds to make the golems fight.

What would even *more* power feel like?

The alarm clock went off at midnight, which seemed like the right time to avoid getting caught by my parents. But it was closer to one o'clock by the time I slipped out of my house, grabbed my bike and rode over to the ravine.

Holding my flashlight in one hand and fighting the buzzing mosquitoes with the other, I carefully zigzagged my way down the narrow path in the bushes until I arrived at the creek bed at the bottom of the ravine.

I checked my phone. Shouldn't Seth be here already?

I figured I might as well get started on my golem.

I set my flashlight down on a stump and pointed it at the creek. It cast a series of freakish shadows against the foliage that gave me goose bumps. Still, my rational mind told me there was nothing to fear in these woods—the only animals living here were squirrels and chipmunks. And besides, my golem could deal with anything bigger. I began to pull mud out of the creek bed. Soon I had fashioned a life-sized clay figure. In the darkness, the thing looked freakish. I'd worked so quickly that the golem was misshapen, with a squashed head and limbs of different lengths.

Just one last detail...

I reached out with my finger and carved the three letters into the golem's head, spelling out emet—truth.

Then I dug into my pocket and pulled out the paper with the new instructions Seth had given me. Once I said the words, the golem would come alive and allow me to enter it.

But no way was I doing any of this without seeing Seth do it first.

And Seth was nowhere to be seen.

What if he'd tried this crazy stunt on his own again? What if something had gone wrong?

This was crazy. I didn't care what Seth had in mind. I decided there was no way I was going to get inside a golem and have some kind of weird monster duel with Seth. Maybe there was a good reason that ancient book had stayed hidden at the back of the synagogue all these years.

Maybe I should just go home. It was the middle of the night. And here I was, deep in the ravine, up to my ankles in creek water.

But what if Seth was in danger?

Maybe I should get help. I'd turned around and taken a few steps away from the golem when I heard it.

A voice almost beyond my hearing range, speaking quietly. In Hebrew.

It was *Seth*.

"Where are you?" I asked, straining to see through the darkness. I doubled back to the stump I'd put the flashlight on. The beam was still pointing at the clay giant I'd fashioned. It was standing still, facing the other side of the creek. I gazed at the lifeless hunk of clay. Somehow it seemed taller than I recalled building it. A trick of the light?

Seth's voice continued, uttering Hebrew phrases that were completely beyond me. Wasn't he supposed to wait until he'd built his own golem before doing the incantation? Wasn't he supposed to come down here and find me?

THE WAY OF THE GOLEM

I reached over to grab the flashlight—

Something was moving!

The golem.

It had leaned forward, its arm outstretched, and was trying to grab hold of me. The clay appendage oozed forward, thick and meaty, less like an arm and more like the tentacle of some sea creature. It tightened around my wrist as more liquid clay bubbled out of the golem's body and enveloped my hand, wrist and forearm. I tried to pull away, but the creature yanked back, throwing me into the shallow water.

I tried to flex my arm, but the cold clay was rippling over me, pulling me back, until I could feel it dripping down my back, running over my head and face.

It had me.

I could feel the liquid clay tightening around my skin everywhere, pulling and pushing at my muscles and forcing me to stand up on my feet against my will.

I gasped for breath and found that Seth had been right. The clay did allow a space for me to breathe, both through my nose and mouth. And there was a small space in front of each eye so I could peer out into the night.

I lifted my foot, and the golem did the same.

So it was true after all. There were instructions to make a person fit into a golem, to control it, only—

Only I hadn't read the instructions. They were still in my pocket, now completely covered with a thick layer of clay. I couldn't get to them even if I wanted to.

The only person who could help me was...

Seth!

He must have activated the golem, but he'd activated mine instead of his. Had he even fashioned one for himself yet? I pivoted and spotted him, illuminated by the glow of the flashlight.

He was holding a book in his hands, still reading aloud, but in a voice that was quiet, nearly under his breath.

Through the clay bubbling around me, I could see that the book in his hands was the same one he'd yanked off the shelf back in the synagogue.

The book he'd taken the golem instructions from.

I took a step in his direction.

Suddenly the clay around me seized, as if someone had slammed on the brakes.

I felt my body pitch forward, but the golem held its place, keeping me from falling onto my face.

Then I felt my left leg lift up against my will. My body pivoted with the movement of the golem.

"What are you doing?" I said. Or *tried* to say. But the golem wouldn't let me. I couldn't control its mouth. All I could do was grunt.

Seth approached. He leaned in close to me.

"You're not very smart," he told me. His voice was different somehow.

"Why are you doing this?" I asked. This time the words came out. It was a bit like talking underwater.

"It's like I told you," Seth said. "I've made golems. Little ones. Big ones. But it all gets so very boring after a while. Dad never understood. Or maybe he understood all too well. Maybe *that's* why he tried to hide that book from me."

"Please, Seth. Let me out of this thing—"

"Quiet," he snapped, putting a finger to my clay-smeared lips. He stared at me.

"I thought we were friends…"

Seth laughed a cruel, bitter laugh. "Friends?" He flicked his hand at me. "You thought we were *friends*? *Us*?"

"But…"

Seth's brow creased and his eyebrows furrowed. He bared his teeth and said harshly, "You never once stood up for me when you were with *them*."

"I tried," I sputtered. "I wanted to…"

"No," Seth said, his voice low and guttural. "You were a coward, Justin. And I never forgot it."

Then he muttered something under his breath.

I tried to open my mouth to speak, but the clay lips didn't move.

"Seth!" I screamed, but all that came out was a muffled, angry gurgle.

I tried to scream again and reach out to give him a left hook—you know, really knock him off his feet—but the clay held me back. All I managed to do was make the golem wobble slightly.

Then Seth leaned in *really* close, so close he was looking me right in the eyes. "It's too bad you never paid attention in Hebrew school, Justin. If you had, you would realize how much power words have. Power to hurt when they're used for teasing, sure, but so much more than that. It's like that word I taught you, *emet*. Truth. We can be truthful, can't we, Justin?"

I tried to scream at him, but he wasn't listening. "Do you know what happens when you erase the aleph? That is to say, the first letter of the word *emet*?"

Even if I'd wanted to answer, Seth was in complete control of the golem, and he wasn't letting me move a muscle.

"Didn't think so," he said with a chuckle. He reached forward, and I felt his hand resting against my forehead. The clay surrounding me felt colder somehow. His thumb pressed firmly into the clay on my forehead, moving back and forth, back and forth.

"No idea?" he said. "Tsk. Tsk. Tsk. If you take away the aleph, you're left with the word *met.*"

Of course, I had no idea what he was talking about. But his words weren't my biggest concern right now. The clay around me was changing. I could feel it in my feet and my fingertips. A tingling sort of feeling, like pins and needles. Only colder, like Seth had jammed icicles under my fingernails.

Wait a minute...the Hebrew lessons were coming back to me. That word—

"That's right," said Seth. "Now you're catching up. *Met.* The Hebrew word for 'death.'"

The tingling was spreading across my face. The clay pulled tighter against my skin. I stood there breathing—or trying to breathe. I was still breathing, right?

The clay was so cold now.

"And you know what?" Seth said, moving away from me and standing just inside my field of vision. "This time *I'm* the one who's going to stand by and watch."

You can't do this! I tried to scream. *I can't move! I don't even think I can breathe!*

Seth backed away, staring at his handiwork with pride. "It's like I told you," he said, his voice going flat. "We are *all* but clay in the hands of our maker."

SCREEN TIME

Isaac's basement was THE BEST BASEMENT EVER.

It was not the newest, not the most renovated and certainly not the cleanest. Junk of all kinds was piled against the walls, in boxes, out of boxes—heck, there were even plain old empty boxes just for the sake of having boxes. Wedged into the mountains of refuse there were some cool toys and games, but the best stuff was a bunch of old electronic equipment that Isaac's dad had collected over the years—VCRs, rotary phones, walkie-talkies, you name it. All manner of tangled wires were coiled across the floor. The place looked like a pit of electronic vipers. It was not the kind of basement you would want to sleep on the floor of, unless you (a) had an aversion to soft beds or (b) wanted to stay up super late watching scary movies on an old TV.

And by "old TV," we're talking about one of those massive tube televisions that professional weightlifters might try hoisting to build up their abs.

Xander nudged Isaac in the ribs. "So what are we gonna watch tonight? Something gory? Something with somebody's head getting ripped off? You know me—I love a good decapitation."

Xander could never get away with watching those kinds of things at his own house. Neither could Isaac usually, but the rules did not seem to apply when you were having a sleepover in the basement.

Xander moved past Isaac, sitting cross-legged on the floor, and over to the weathered cardboard box in the corner, which had a mass of thick extension cords piled on top of it. They'd discovered it a couple of weeks back. Maybe Isaac's dad knew the kids had found out about the box, maybe he didn't. Maybe he had decided to honor the unwritten rule of the basement: what's *found* in the basement *stays* in the basement, no questions asked.

Xander pushed the cords off the box and looked inside. The treasure within almost gleamed at him under the hanging bulbs that lit the room.

He was staring down at a heap of old videocassettes, some still in their boxes, some lying naked with no labels to identify them. Most of them were horror films, judging by the lurid cover art—*The Cincinnati Ripper, Grave Ghouls, Severed Head* and Dead...trash to some, but classics to Isaac and Xander. They had been slowly working their way through them.

"We could watch *Grave Ghouls* again," said Xander.

Isaac, not even looking up, said, "Nah, the effects suck."

"I wonder what else your dad's got hidden around here," Xander mused.

"Dude, you start moving boxes around and you're going to cause an avalanche," Isaac said. He waved to the mountains of piles. "One false move and we'll be buried alive in all this crap."

But Xander was already shuffling stuff around. "Hello! What's this?" He leaned forward and scooped up something that had been behind the box of videos.

Isaac got up, curious. He had scoured the basement more times than he cared to remember and knew the contents well. There was nothing that could surprise him, but what had piqued Xander's interest?

Xander turned around and brandished the large object in his hands. It was an old video camera, the kind you had to rest on your shoulder, like TV newspeople often used. It could fit one of those big old videotapes and had a long lens that jutted out like a telescope. Xander waved it at Isaac. "You have been holding out on me, man! We could have been using this to make zombie movies. Or light stuff on fire and record it. I mean, I guess we could have been doing all of that with our cell-phone cameras. But this is totally old-school." He was really stoked.

Isaac blinked. "I've never seen that camera before," he said. He pulled it out of Xander's hands. The thing was *heavy*. It was definitely old. Really old, like, from the eighties. But Isaac was certain that it hadn't been in the basement for long. For starters, he would have noticed it by now. "It's not even covered in dust," he found himself muttering.

Isaac hit a button, and a panel on the side of the camera popped open. He pulled out the videotape that was inside. Like the ones in the box, it was rectangular and had two spools on the back that rotated a film of magnetic tape around the cassette. What roused Isaac's interest, though, was the label stuck to the front. It was old and faded and had started to peel. It looked like it had already been reglued on. The label had just a series of names on it—Davis, Michael, Anthony, Melanie—all written with different pens in different hand-writing, and all crossed out.

But that's not what had caught Isaac's attention. It was the last name, which hadn't been crossed out and which Isaac knew well. "Richard," he said quietly.

"Hey, that's your *dad's* name," Xander announced in a voice that Isaac suddenly found too loud for some reason.

Isaac shot a glance at the empty staircase leading upstairs. Then his eyes fell back to the tape. "It's also in his handwriting," Isaac admitted.

"Weird. We should totally watch that tape," Xander said.

Isaac looked over at the stairwell again. "I wonder why all those other names are crossed off."

"It's probably just an old tape your dad recorded stuff onto. And there were no other stickers around," offered Xander. "So he just recorded over the last thing on the tape, crossed the old name off the list and wrote his name on it."

"But why wouldn't he just write what he'd actually recorded on the tape? Why even use an old tape to record things?" countered Isaac.

"I don't know, man. But really, who cares?" Xander snatched the tape out of Isaac's hands. "Obviously, your dad likes old tech. He likes playing with ancient video cameras. And, obviously, he put something cool on this tape, and we are going to watch it."

Isaac didn't say or do anything as Xander took the video and placed it into the VCR under the old TV. Part of him was thinking that this might not be the best idea, that there might be something private on that tape he shouldn't be seeing. But the other part of him, the curious part that was egging Xander on, stood back and let him set it up.

"Okay, it's ready," Xander said. He pressed the Play button.

The screen lit up and buzzed with black-and-white static.

Isaac breathed a quiet sigh of relief.

Xander shook his head. "Maybe we have to rewind the tape or fast-forward it or something."

As he got up to investigate, the static was silenced by a white line that ran down the screen. A wobbly image appeared of Isaac's dad. You could tell from the background that the footage had been recorded here in the basement. Isaac's dad had clearly positioned the camera on top of the TV and aimed it right where the boys were sitting now.

"Just like I figured," Xander said. "It's a movie your dad made. Of himself. Is that guy vain or what?"

Isaac narrowed his eyes. There was more to it than that. There were little bits of static pulsing over the image, and blips and lines running up and down the screen—probably because the tape had been used and reused so many times. Videotape was magnetic—Isaac's dad had told him all about it—and the more you used it, the weaker the signal became.

But why was his dad just sitting there staring into the camera? How was that something worth recording?

"Isaac," said the image on the screen.

Isaac jumped back.

Xander looked over at his friend and let out a big laugh. "Look at you! You're white as a ghost!"

"Isaac, Xander, it's *me*," said Isaac's dad, leaning closer to the camera.

Xander and Isaac looked at each other.

For a second Xander looked like he was going to scream, but then it hit him. "Oh, I get it. Nice one, Mr. Lazar."

Isaac just stared at the screen. "Dad?"

"It's very convincing," Xander admitted. "But don't you see? Your dad is pranking us. He knows we've been watching the scary movies in that box. He knew we'd go looking for more. He knew we'd find the camera and a tape that makes it *seem* like your dad is speaking to us in real time or something."

He stood up and pointed at the TV set. "I call your bluff, Mr. Lazar!"

"Xander, stop goofing around and sit your butt down this instant," Isaac's onscreen dad said. "I need you to listen to me."

"Holy crap," Xander said. "He's really got these beats figured out. He knows exactly when we're going to speak, and how long to pause in between. This might be the best practical joke of all time. Impressive!"

"I am trying to warn you," Isaac's dad said, his voice grave. "You're in a lot of danger."

Xander shrugged this off, but Isaac put his hands up to the screen. "Dad? Is that you? What are you doing in there?"

"No, Isaac," Xander snapped. "He's not in the TV set. You just watched *Poltergeist* too many times when you were a kid. And your dad knows it."

"Xander," the image onscreen said, "for once in your life, I need you to shut up so I can explain."

"Sure, sure," Xander said, putting his hands behind his head. "Whatever you say."

Onscreen Dad switched his gaze from Xander to Isaac. "Listen, I found the camera and the tapes at a garage sale a few weeks ago. I started to pore over the contents tape by tape."

"You mean that box with all the cords on top?" Isaac asked.

"Yes—"

"Some awesome flicks in there, Mr. L."

Isaac shot Xander an irritated look.

"Boys, there isn't time to explain it all now, but you need to understand one thing. *I'm* the real me."

"Of course you're the real you," said Xander.

"No, you don't understand. There's only one of me, and I'm here, trapped on the tape."

"Hilarious," Xander said.

"Shut up, Xander!" Isaac elbowed Xander in the ribs. "What do you mean?" he whispered at the screen. "Who's that upstairs then?"

Onscreen Dad leaned in close and spoke very quietly. "It's the recording. My copy. A copy of me. It's almost perfect, and now it wants to replace me. It has replaced all of the others on the tape and probably erased them. You'll see in a moment—there are more tapes, which means there are more copies. Copies of *people*."

"I don't understand," Isaac said, feeling his heartbeat thudding faster. He reached out and tried to put his hand through the screen, but it just clunked against the glass screen.

"No, I'm not *in* the set," Onscreen Dad said. He waved his hands in the air. "Somehow this is all that's left of me for the time being. And I'm vulnerable. Listen carefully. Here's what I need you to do. This is very important. I need you to switch the tape off now. Put it someplace safe. We'll find a way to reverse the process, so that I can get back into my body. That man upstairs is just…an *analog* copy of me. But he…if you want to think of *it* as a *he*…won't want to go back on the tape. He's tricked all the others before me. He tricked me too, and he'll trick you if you're not careful—"

Onscreen Dad suddenly stopped talking. His eyes flitted to something beyond the space where Xander and Isaac were sitting. His mouth dropped open. "Oh no," he said.

"Gotcha!" a voice called out.

Xander and Isaac whirled around. Xander screamed.

It was Isaac's dad—his *real* dad, the dad in corporeal form—just a few paces behind them.

He was standing with his hands on his hips. He had an amused grin on his face.

Onscreen Dad shook his head. "Quickly," he said. "Before it's too late."

Isaac's dad smiled. "You fell for it."

"What do you mean?" Xander asked, eyes moving back and forth from the image onscreen to the man standing in front of them.

"My joke," Isaac's dad said, not looking at the boys. He was too busy ejecting the tape from the video camera. Onscreen Dad—his face frozen with terror—suddenly disappeared, and the screen reverted to static.

There was only one Isaac's dad left in the room, and he was holding the video recording of Onscreen Dad in his hands. He quietly inspected the magnetic spools for a moment. Then he eyed the boys. "Pretty good, right? I *totally* got you!"

Isaac didn't say anything.

Xander nodded. He gave a laugh, but it was shaky and weak. "Yeah, that's right. You got us," he said, his eyes locked on the tape.

Then Isaac's dad dropped the video cassette. There was an audible crunch. "Whoops."

"Dad?" Isaac said.

Isaac's dad bent over and picked up the tape. "Silly me," he said. "I've gone and *broken* the thing." Then he flipped a hinge on the top of the cassette and pulled out a long ribbon of black tape as if he were pulling off a ream of dental floss. He snapped it off and yanked a few more times, until he'd removed several feet of tape. The black ribbon dangled in the air and then fell limply to the floor.

"Dad?" Isaac said again, staring from the tape to the man standing before them.

"Oh, don't worry, son," Isaac's dad said. "I've got plenty more tapes. You know me and my passion for collecting."

He made his way over to the corner and pulled another cassette out of the box. Isaac got only a quick glance, but he saw that it also had a label on the side. A series of words, all crossed out. His dad popped the cassette into the camera.

Then he picked up the camera, mounted it on his shoulder and turned toward Isaac and Xander, who just sat there, frozen.

"Okay, boys," he said, aiming the lens right at them. "Let me show you how this thing works."

SWEET AS PIE

The pie smelled good. Yasmin wasn't necessarily a fan of pumpkin pie, but this one called to her. She came to the weekend farmers' market every once in a while, usually to shop for overpriced organic vegetables with her parents. They said it was important to help the local growers, although Yasmin had noticed that her folks were not above buying fruits and berries shipped from halfway around the world. Her dad did love his bananas.

Random thoughts like these tried to pull her away from the pumpkin pie, but it was stronger than anything her brain could cook up.

The pie stood out from the other items at the farmer's stall. It almost shone, with a bright-orange hue more like the bold color of a pumpkin itself as opposed to the darker, richer tones of a normal pumpkin pie. Food coloring, perhaps?

There were other things on display: some unhusked corn, a few bins of apples, a couple varieties of squash—the usual fall-harvest fare. Yasmin diverted her attention from the pie to the woman in the booth selling it.

"How much?" Yasmin asked, digging into her pocket. Darn it. She hadn't brought any money.

"For you?" the woman said, smiling. "It's on the house."

Yasmin blinked. "Really?"

"Just one thing," the woman added.

"What's that?"

"Be sure to tell all your friends about us. Ryland Farms. We're just outside of town, first concession past Highway 6."

Yasmin nodded blankly. The smell of the pie was overpowering. All she could think about was cramming as much of it into her face as quickly as possible. It smelled so good she wished there were more of it, so she could smother her face in it completely.

It took only seconds to scarf the whole pie down. She thought she would want more, but as soon as she'd swallowed the last crumb, Yasmin realized she was quite satisfied. Not disgustingly full, as she should have felt after eating enough pie for six, but just right.

She took a deep breath and dabbed at her cheeks with the napkin the farmer had given her.

"Pretty good, right?" the farmer said. She didn't seem at all alarmed by what she'd just seen.

Yasmin felt herself flush. She had only just realized that she'd made a complete pig of herself in front of this woman she did not know. "Pretty good," Yasmin said, not knowing how to explain her actions.

"You be sure to tell your friends," the woman insisted.

"Ryland Farms," Yasmin said, looking around the stall. "You haven't got a sign up though."

"Oh, we're always here," the woman beamed. "Every Sunday morning."

Yasmin nodded and moved away from the stall. Even though she'd been to the market many times, she had never seen that woman before. But maybe other farmers had manned the booth, and the stall had just blended in with all the rest.

Yasmin gave no more thought to the farmer, the pie or the market for the rest of the day. It was Sunday, and that meant thinking about completing her homework but watching something on Netflix instead, then talking to her friends on the phone, maybe helping herself to a snack and doing all the other mindless things Sundays seemed designed for.

It was only when she was getting ready to wash up that night that Yasmin noticed her left hand. Something seemed off.

She couldn't place it though. She held her hands up to the light and examined the fingers on one hand and then the other.

"What's wrong, Yasmin?" her mother asked, entering the bathroom and noticing Yasmin staring at her left hand.

"Do my fingers look a bit...*yellow* to you?" Jasmine asked.

Her mother looked at each finger on Yasmin's left hand. Then she held them up to the light. "You must have gotten ink on them. It'll come off with a good scrub."

But it didn't come out in the washing. If anything, scrubbing her fingers only made the color stand out more, to the point where they no longer seemed yellow but *orange*.

Yes, *orange*.

The same orange, in fact, as that pumpkin pie she'd eaten.

It made Yasmin think of the movie *Charlie and the Chocolate Factory* and the girl who tried the gum that changed flavors. It got stuck on blueberry-pie flavor, and she turned into a bright-blue ball and got wheeled off. Ridiculous, of course, but that girl had gone *so* blue, and now the fingers on Yasmin's left hand were *so* orange...

Nah. Maybe it was an allergic reaction?

"A rash," her mother said. "I've had something like that before," she added, eyeing the orange tint to Yasmin's fingers. "It'll clear up."

"Should we call the doctor or something?"

Yasmin's mother made her thoughtful face. Yasmin knew what her mother was thinking. That the doctor's office was already closed for the day. Was this alarming enough to trek all the way to the walk-in clinic? "Does it hurt?" her mother asked.

Yasmin didn't want to spend three hours in the waiting room, probably with no Wi-Fi, which is what would happen if she said yes. And the truth of it was, her fingers didn't hurt. They felt okay, only...

Now it was Yasmin's turn to make a face. She curled her fingers, which felt tighter somehow. Dry even. She rubbed her hands together. She swore she heard the skin crackling, but maybe some moisturizer would fix that. "I'll be all right," she said.

Her mother sighed, and Yasmin could hear the relief. "We'll sleep on it," she said. "See how you're feeling in the morning."

Yasmin woke up feeling just fine.

Her alarm clock blared to life, and Yasmin slowly opened her eyes. She stretched a bit, trying to wake her body. That's when she felt it.

Something dry and crumbly was under the covers. It felt like someone had shoved a small pile of dry leaves into the bed.

She tried to pull back the sheets, but the fingers on her left hand couldn't grab hold of them.

She must have fallen asleep on her hand or something. The pins and needles would pass in a moment, as long as she flexed her fingers to let the blood start pumping to her extremities again.

Still no feeling. With her other hand, Yasmin reached over to her bedside table to turn on the table lamp, and—

She screamed.

Probably not for too long, but loudly enough for her mother and father to come flying into her room.

"What's wrong? What is it?"

Yasmin opened her mouth to speak, but no sound came out. With her free hand, she motioned to the withered stump that used to be her left hand.

Her mother shook her head. "No, no, no…"

All three of them stared at Yasmin's hand in horror. Dried and crumpled, with all the fluid sucked dry, her fingers were now just empty brown husks. Two of them had crumpled into little pieces that were already making a mess of her sheets, but the others still retained the shape and form of her former fleshy fingers.

"No, no, no," her mother said again.

Her father said, "Put on your things. We're going to the hospital."

"I've never seen anything quite like it before," the doctor said.

That was the not the sort of thing Yasmin wanted to hear.

"What do you mean *never*?" her mother gasped.

But the doctor ignored Yasmin's mother, narrowing his eyes and staring through his bifocals at the nub of dried flesh that used to be Yasmin's hand. He prodded at it with his hand, which was covered in a latex glove.

"Does it hurt?"

"No," Yasmin said, shaking her head. She could feel tears starting to well up. Her hand! Her hand was *gone*!

She clenched the fingers of her right hand—the only one left—to try to hold back the scream. She clenched so hard that her nails dug into the soft flesh of her palm and drew blood.

The doctor hadn't even noticed.

Yasmin watched as he moved away from her hand, examining the contents of the plastic bag that had been brought to him. It contained the last bits and pieces of Yasmin's hand, the fingers that were no longer fingers and more like dried—

"Leaves," the doctor said, finishing Yasmin's thought. "That's what this looks like. Dried autumn leaves."

Now he turned to face Yasmin, looking at the stump on her wrist and then back to the bag in his hand. He squinted, as if noticing something important.

"What is it?" Yasmin said, her voice sharp, her breath quick.

"I can't believe I'm even saying this, but take a close look at what's left of the fingernails."

The doctor held out the bag to Yasmin and her parents. "You see it, don't you?"

"What are we supposed to be looking at?!" Yasmin's father snapped.

"The nails," the doctor said, pointing to the white ovals at the tips of Yasmin's shriveled fingers.

"They're *gone*, we know that!"

"They're not nails," the doctor said. "I could almost swear…they look more like…" He stopped himself, shaking his head in disbelief. "…like *pumpkin* seeds."

"This is the place, Yasmin," her mother said, looking at the address on her phone. "Ryland Farms."

Already it was nearly dark. Getting released from the hospital hadn't been easy. Yasmin had had to promise to come back in the morning to see the specialist.

But how long did she have, really?

Already the fingers of her other hand were turning orange and…crumbly.

Yasmin stared out the car window. A dilapidated old house overlooked a cornfield. It probably looked beautiful at some times of year. Yasmin tried to imagine the tall green stalks of corn swaying under a gentle breeze. But the corn had been cut, and the stalks were broken and yellow.

Yasmin opened the car door. How long did she have until her fingers on her right hand withered off and she wouldn't be able to do something as basic as opening a door or even holding a pencil?

There were answers here—she was sure of it. She would find out what had caused this and then get back to the hospital, and the doctors would find some kind of solution. Maybe they would be able to reverse the process.

Or...

Or stop it.

Yes, Yasmin told herself, to keep from panicking. The doctors would find some clue in the DNA of the pumpkin, figure out how to slow down this quick vegetable rot that was taking over her body, and stop it.

Yasmin started to get out of the car. A harsh breeze tried to slam the door back on her, but she kicked the door open and spilled out onto the ground.

She hoisted herself back up and marched toward the house. Her mother and father followed her.

"You're sure this is the place?" her dad asked, looking at his phone. "We have to be sure before we call the police. We don't want a repeat of what happened when we had them contact the farmers' market..."

They'd been told there was no Ryland Farms. That it had never had a stall at the farmers' market. The police did say that if Yasmin or her family found any kind of evidence, they could contact an officer for follow-up. Not before. And so here they were, looking for evidence.

But even as she went to bang on the door, Yasmin knew they would not find anyone inside. The place was empty. She could hear the wind whistling through the cracks in the roof.

"There's no Ryland Farms," she said, her voice faltering.

Her dad turned on his cell-phone light and tried pointing it through a window into one of the dank rooms. "I'll search around the house," he said.

Yasmin nodded. "I'll go around back."

Her mother close behind, Yasmin paced around the corner of the house. It was unlikely she was going to find anything but more chopped corn stalks. She did find something though.

Scarecrows.

There were six or seven of them, but they looked like they'd been unattended for quite some time, not because a murder of crows had roosted on them, but because they were unfinished.

Headless, in fact.

The scarecrows stood there, all in strangely angular positions, the wind whipping at their clothes and revealing the rotting straw and other organic matter used for stuffing. It was hard to see more detail in the darkening sky. The sun had already set, and there were only minutes left of natural light.

Even so, Yasmin spotted what the scarecrows had been left to guard.

Pumpkins. A whole field full of them.

"I knew it!" Yasmin said, walking toward the field. She turned to her mother and tried to call her over with the stump of her left hand. It had always been her dominant hand, and she still relied on it from instinct.

But her mother just stood there, shaking her head.

"No, I'm serious, Mom. This is it. The pumpkin patch. It's where the pumpkins in that pie came from. It *has* to be."

"Yasmin, come *back*," her mother urged. She would not come any closer.

There wasn't time to argue.

Yasmin needed answers. She walked into the patch to get a better look at the pumpkins. Many were lying at the feet of those scarecrows. Some were the bright-orange color of the pie she'd eaten. Some were darker.

Except...Yasmin noticed that they weren't *just* pumpkins.

She bent down to inspect one more closely. "It can't be," she said.

She was staring at a jack-o-lantern. Scanning the pumpkins on the damp earth, Yasmin could see that they were *all* jack-o-lanterns. Pumpkins that had been designed to look like faces. But these were not your standard "carve out a toothy grin and two eyes" type of jack-o-lanterns. These were clearly the work of some kind of brilliant artist, who'd given them features that were almost human. Almost...

And that's when Yasmin realized what was happening.

She stood up.

She began to back away.

"No..." Yasmin said, but already she could feel her head sway. It tipped from side to side, growing heavy. Too heavy for her neck to support. Like it was going to fall to the ground—

Yasmin heard her mother scream.

And then she heard nothing at all.

THE SEARCH ENGINE

Julie should have guessed there was going to be trouble when she agreed to join Francesca Rabuano and Millie Martin. The two of them did nothing but giggle and gossip. Miss O'Doyle had split up those girls early on in the school year, but since Julie sat between them, she'd been stuck passing their notes back and forth.

Julie never passed notes herself, mainly because nobody thought to pass her any. She had friends, like Amelia and Mei Yu, but they were both in Mrs. Weidner's room next door. Francesca and Millie were loud—and *fun*. Julie had wished that maybe they'd let her hang out with them at recess or something, but she'd felt weird about asking. In the meantime, she had just kept passing their notes and trying not to seem like too much of a geek in front of them.

She had always caught little glimpses of the secrets Francesca and Millie scrawled on the paper. Most were about other kids in the class, such as who liked who, or offered juicy gossip, like spotting Miss O'Doyle in town holding hands with Mr. Leblanc, the French teacher. But then Millie passed a note to Julie that wasn't for Francesca. It was for her.

Come with us to the library. Ask Miss O if we can use the computers.

Getting permission to go down to the library was easy. Julie was in Miss O'Doyle's good books because she was quiet and didn't talk back like most of the class did.

Miss O'Doyle had smiled when Julie raised her hand and asked if the girls could go to the library to do research on their ancient-civilizations project. "You can keep an eye on Francesca and Millie for me," she had said with a wink.

So that was it. They'd only asked Julie along so Miss O'Doyle would let them all go. Oh well, it was a start.

Millie and Francesca raced down the stairs, flung open the library door and plopped down at the row of computers lining the far side of the library. Julie followed them and slid into the spot beside Francesca.

She had just nicely logged in when she heard somebody approach.

"You're Julie Lowther," said Ms. Winters, the school librarian. She was as frosty as her name suggested. Even her hair looked like it had been shaved from a block of ice.

Julie looked up from the computer. "Yes?"

"You have a book that's three weeks overdue." Ms. Winters swiveled around and paced back to the checkout desk. Without missing a beat, she grabbed hold of the electronic wand and started checking in books.

"What an old bag," Francesca whispered. "She gives me the creeps."

"She looks like a vampire," Millie chimed in. "She's as dusty as the books in this place. I bet *she* lost your book and is just blaming you."

Julie didn't say anything. She didn't like saying mean things about people, not even Ms. Winters.

The relative silence of the library was broken as Millie started to giggle. Of course, Francesca then joined in. Whenever the two of them started giggling, it was nearly impossible to stop them. Julie leaned over to see what they were up to.

Millie was pointing at the monitor. "I wonder what happens when you type Ms. Winters's name into the search engine," Millie said. "I bet you get a picture of a bat—"

"Or snow and ice?" Julie said, trying to join in.

Millie and Francesca stopped laughing. Julie's stomach tightened. The two girls just stared at her like she was from another planet.

Julie's face went red. "Because, uh, her last name is Winters. You know, like the season?" But still the two girls just kept staring.

"I wonder what happens if we look up *my* name?" Francesca said, moving on to her favorite subject.

She typed in her name and hit the Image Search button. The screen immediately filled with several small thumbnail images of different women, some of them quite old.

"Ugh!" Millie exclaimed. "That's gross." She started typing. "Okay, let's see what I look like."

A whole bunch of images popped up on her screen. "Wow," Millie said, starting to giggle again, "it looks like I'm a cheerleader for some college football team. Nice!"

Francesca and Millie both turned to Julie. "Your turn," they said in unison.

Julie froze. "Uh, aren't we supposed to be doing research?"

Millie rolled her eyes. "Yeah, we will. But first let's see what you get."

Julie sighed. If that's what it would take to get them to accept her, then that's what it would take. She opened the browser and typed in her full name: *Julie Lowther*.

The screen filled with all sorts of pictures. As Julie expected, there were lots of other people who shared her name. She scanned them. Most were women her mom's age. Nobody she knew. "See," Julie said, motioning to the screen, "it's just the same as yours—"

Julie stopped in mid-sentence. She leaned closer to the screen and squinted. A thumbnail image in the bottom left of the screen had caught her attention. It was a picture of a girl sitting in a school library like the one Julie was in, wearing clothes very similar to the ones she had on. Beside her were two girls who looked exactly like Francesca and Millie.

Julie clicked on the image. Instead of the bigger version of the image coming up, the screen displayed a small red X. Julie hit the backspace key. The other images from her search were still there, but that one photograph was gone. She turned to Millie and Francesca. "You saw that picture, didn't you?"

Francesca leaned over and eyed the photo of an older woman wearing a polyester leisure suit. "*That* one? Yikes! I'd say someone is in desperate need of a makeover."

Julie shook her head. "No, not that one. The other one. The one of us."

"There are no pictures of us on there," Millie said. She gave Julie that "Are you an alien?" look again.

Julie typed her full name into the search engine again, hit the Enter key and waited. The screen filled with all sorts of Julie Lowthers, old and young, but not the one she had seen moments earlier. Julie frowned.

"Okay," Francesca said, "we'd better get some work done or else O'Doyle will never let us down here again."

Julie tried typing her name in one last time. She decided she must have imagined the image.

The next day Miss O'Doyle sent Julie down to the library to work on her project without Millie and Francesca. The two of them had gotten into a big argument at recess over an Instagram pic (it was unclear who had done what), and it had spilled over into class. They weren't going anywhere. Instead Miss O'Doyle sent James Gunderson down with her. Julie had always found James a bit odd. He only ever talked about what level he had reached in his online zombie-hunting game. He also hummed a lot, but in general he was harmless.

Ms. Winters pounced on Julie as soon as she entered. "Let me guess," she said, without even a hello. "You forgot the book."

Julie's eyes went wide. "I'm sorry, Ms. Winters. I will bring it back. I promise."

"Promises are things we keep," Ms. Winters said with a scowl.

"I'll write a note and remind myself," Julie replied. "I'll bring it in tomorrow." She waited for the foul expression on Ms. Winters's face to lift. It did not. "Can I use the computer?"

"We use computers for research and schoolwork here," the librarian said coldly.

"Yes," Julie answered. "I'm working on my ancient-civilizations project."

"Yesterday it looked to me like you were talking with your friends and horsing around on the internet."

"No, that was just…" Julie stopped. Ms. Winters was the least understanding person in the school. But she was right. "I promise I'll focus just on my work."

It didn't look as if Ms. Winters was going to let her pass. But just then Mrs. Johnson came in with several little kindergarten students. Ms. Winters turned and marched back to the front desk.

Boy, was that woman ever sour!

Julie made her way to the row of desktop computers and plopped herself down in a seat. James was already working away. Julie logged in to her account and tried to ignore the humming sounds.

She started searching for websites about the ancient Romans. After a half hour or so she'd filled out nearly a full page of notes in her workbook. But her mind began to wander. She started thinking about the image search from the day before and the spooky picture.

It was ridiculous, of course. Nobody could take an image of a person and post it online immediately like that, could they?

She looked over her shoulder.

Ms. Winters was busy checking out books for the kindergarten class.

Julie typed in the words *Julie Lowther*. She hit the Enter key.

The screen filled with thumbnails of all the other Julie Lowthers: the one in the leisure suit, the octogenarian, the one who looked like she starred in some cheesy TV show, the one sitting in the library who looked just like her—

Julie's hand gripped the mouse.

No!

She shot a glance over her shoulder again. Ms. Winters was busy arranging books on the library cart. She looked over her other shoulder. James Gunderson was typing away at the keyboard. Julie leaned in close to the monitor.

It was clearly the picture she'd seen the day before. She *hadn't* imagined it! But hang on a second…She squinted at the screen.

The picture was *almost* the same. It had been taken from the same angle, from the far end of the library, and showed her leaning over the desk, staring at the screen. It was definitely a picture of her, this Julie Lowther, in the library.

But Millie and Francesca were nowhere to be seen. And the girl in the picture was wearing *exactly what Julie was wearing. Today.*

Julie wanted to click on the thumbnail to get a better look, but the last time she had tried that, the picture vanished. Instead, she clicked the button on the left-hand side of the web page. A drop-down menu of options appeared.

Julie clicked the button that said *Sort by date*. Immediately the pictures on the screen rearranged themselves. The little picture of Julie came up first, with the caption *Taken in the last hour* below it.

Impossible.

Julie looked around. "Hey, psst! James!"

James looked over at Julie. "Huh?"

"Come here. I need to show you something."

"Like what?"

"This picture. Please, James. It's important!"

"Oh, all right," James muttered and rolled his chair over to Julie's desk. "What am I supposed to be looking at?"

"There, the picture…"

"Of what? You typed your name into the search engine. Big deal. There's tons of them."

"Yeah, but look at *that* one," Julie said, tapping the monitor with her finger.

But the picture had vanished. The page must have refreshed while Julie was trying to get James's attention.

"You know, you're supposed to be doing your work," James said matter-of-factly.

"I would agree!" a voice snapped from behind.

Julie nearly leaped from her seat. "Ms. Winters!" she exclaimed.

"Julie Lowther," Ms. Winters replied. "And obviously you know your own name well, since you've been typing it into the search engine."

"No, Ms. Winters, it's just that—"

"James," Ms. Winters continued, "please go back to your seat."

"Now you're in for it," muttered James. Julie watched James roll back to his station.

"I don't need to remind you again about acceptable use of school technology, do I?" the librarian asked. It wasn't really a question. For a moment it looked as if she might say something else, but then she turned and silently glided back to her desk.

Julie let out a shaky sigh. Fine. She'd do her research. She could investigate the images more when she was at home and on her own time. She typed *Ancient Roman architecture* into the search engine, and a long list of websites filled the page.

Julie clicked on the first one.

A series of thumbnail images popped up. Most were pictures of aqueducts and the Colosseum. There were paintings, too, and photographs of actual ruins. But at the very bottom of the page Julie spotted a picture of herself in the library.

She tried to swallow, but her mouth had gone dry.

She leaned in and studied the image carefully. It was nearly the same picture she had seen a few minutes earlier, but not quite. This one was taken at a closer angle. It was a picture of her leaning over the computer just as she was *right now*.

Julie pushed her chair back and bolted up. She paced around the library, looking for a clue. There had to be a camera in the room. Had to be! Someone—maybe Millie and Francesca—had been taking pictures and uploading them. All they needed was a cell phone and internet access. That's it. That was the explanation.

Julie marched over to Ms. Winters. "Excuse me," she said.

Ms. Winters gave her a cold stare. "What is it now?"

"Are there cameras in the library?" Julie asked. She was trying not to let on how scared she was, but the words came out all shaky.

"Cameras in the library?" Ms. Winters repeated. There was a curious tone to her voice that Julie couldn't figure out. Did Ms. Winters know something?

No, that was ridiculous. She was a mean old bat, but Julie didn't think she'd be involved in something like this.

"Never mind," said Julie. She didn't take her eyes off Ms. Winters. She just backed away and slipped into her seat. Then she stared at the screen.

The picture had vanished. All the images were related to ancient Rome.

Julie's head was pounding. And all she could hear was James humming. And the smashing of computer keys like his fingertips were hammers.

"Stop it!" Julie snapped.

James looked at her, surprised.

Julie leaped out of her seat and stood over his shoulder. "It's not you doing this, is it?" She searched for any sign of a camera or a program James might be using to upload pictures. All she saw was some dumb website about Roman warfare.

"You're so weird, Julie. I'm outta here."

James stood up, turned off the computer, collected his things and left.

Julie hung her head. She went back to the computer.

She typed in her name again. *Julie Lowther.*

The screen was full of thumbnail images, but none were of the fashionable or old or famous Julie Lowthers. They were

all of her, here in the library, leaning over the desk and staring at the computer.

They weren't all the same though. Julie strained to pick out the differences. As she scanned the first row of images, she noticed how the camera angles kept changing. Someone was moving the camera closer and closer to her.

Julie looked over her shoulder.

Ms. Winters had disappeared into her office. The door was closed. It was just her, alone, in the library. There was no one else here.

Julie whipped her head back toward the monitor.

The muscles around her eyes twitched. She scanned the next row of images.

Same thing. The camera was getting closer. Julie scanned the pictures so quickly that they all blurred and seemed to move. It was like watching the pages of a flipbook come to life.

The pictures were *here*, happening *now*. Whoever was holding the camera was right behind her. Right at her back. Inches away from her throat—

Julie reached the end of the web page. She sat there, gasping for breath. Her hands were so sweaty she could barely keep her grip on the mouse.

Her eyes were drawn to the bright-blue arrow at the bottom corner of the web page.

There was another page, still waiting for her.

What Julie *wanted* to do was turn off the computer, get up and walk back to class. It was almost recess. She could talk to Miss O'Doyle about what had just happened. *Somebody* would help her.

But instead Julie clicked on the arrow.

The page refreshed.

One lone row of thumbnails appeared.

Julie scanned the images. As she studied each one, she noticed that the picture Julie was slowly turning her head. A look of surprise came over her, and then it quickly changed to one of horror.

Julie had never seen a human face look so utterly terrified. Her eyes were wide. Her lips were pulled back across her face. If a picture could scream, this last one would shatter glass.

The rest of the page was just a blank white screen. There was nothing else.

Shakily Julie switched off the monitor. The room was spinning around her, but she didn't dare move her head.

"Ms. Winters?" Julie called out, her voice as thin as paper.

A deafening silence answered her.

"Hello?"

Nothing.

Ms. Winters might be in her office, or halfway around the world. She would not hear Julie. And there was no one else here.

Julie just sat there, frozen with fear. What should she do?

The recess bell rang.

Julie jumped, her heart in her throat. She heard the thunder of footsteps rain down the hallway, heard the screams of excited kids as they spilled out into the yard. The sound faded, and once again Julie was alone.

She wiped the stinging tears from her eyes. She took a deep breath.

And then she turned around.

BROKEN RECORD

"So what do you think?" Jared's grandfather asked.

Jared stood outside the house. He was supposed to be staring at it, because his grandfather was so proud of it, but how could he ignore the view?

The house was perched like an eagle's nest in the midst of the mountain range. Before him were vast, jutting cliffs of angled rock. A few pine trees flecked whatever surface they could jab their roots into. To find signs of a more habitable space, you had to peer far below.

It was like looking down at the whole world, Jared thought. He felt like one of those Norse gods who lived way up on the mountaintop in Asgard. He'd been to this site a couple of times before and had felt the same way each time. On his last visit, while the house was still being built, Jared could see all the way down to the village below, where the cars were so tiny they looked like rows of ants. It had been such a clear day that Jared could see all the way to the ocean, a blue line at the very edge of the horizon.

But today clouds were rolling in. They began to blanket the view of the village. Soon all Jared could spot were a few craggy peaks of surrounding mountains and the layer of fluffy cloud beneath him.

Jared's grandfather was proud of his new property.

Building the house had not been easy. For starters, there was the road to get there, a series of zigzagging switchbacks with tight curves. You didn't just build a straight road up the side of a mountain. For starters, it would be too steep to drive your car up it.

Plus, even if you did manage to zoom up the side of the mountain, you wouldn't have time to acclimatize to the altitude. The air this high up was cooler and thinner. Each time Jared had arrived here, he'd felt light-headed. Actually, it was more like someone had cracked open his skull, stuck a spoon in his mind and churned it around until he felt like puking.

Getting from the base of the mountain to the peak took at least twenty minutes.

But so worth the drive—what a house!

The inside of the place was just as impressive as the view. Jared's grandfather had made his money in construction. He built big timber-framed houses, and this was his masterpiece. The frame of the house was literally made from whole tree trunks that had been hacked and sawed so they fit together like massive Lego pieces.

A lot of money had been spent on the floor-to-ceiling windows that allowed for as complete a view of the surroundings as you could get.

"Well, what do you think?" Jared's grandfather asked again once they were inside.

Jared dug into his pocket and pulled out his cell phone. He snapped a few photos of the place. He was about to send one to his dad and then a horrible truth dawned upon him. "There's no cell reception up here," Jared said, dismayed.

Jared's grandfather shook his head.

"How am I supposed to, you know, talk to anyone?" Oh man, he thought, this is going to be a long weekend without Wi-Fi.

"I thought you came here to hang out with me," his grandfather said.

Jared's face flushed. "I did, Grandpa, but...you know..."

"I know many things. What specifically were you referring to?"

Jared shrugged. "I wanted to be able to talk to my friends."

Jared's grandfather cracked a small, sly grin. "Any of them happen to be girls?"

Jared didn't say anything. But he felt his face flush a deeper shade of red.

"Is she cute?"

Jared licked his lips. "Yeah, she's all right."

"What's her name?"

"It's..." Jared realized he was already telling his grandfather more than he had told his own parents. "Her name's Olivia.

She's a year older than me, and she doesn't really know I exist. Not in person, I mean."

"This girl you like. *Olivia*. She likes music?"

Jared shrugged.

"You've got a thing for shrugging, don't you?"

Jared shrugged again.

"Here," Jared's grandfather said, walking to a corner of the main room that didn't have windows. There was a shelf with two massive speakers, and a box with a circular platform. A turntable, Jared realized. It was what DJs and old dudes like his grandfather listened to music on.

Jared's grandfather reached up to a shelf above the turntable and ran his finger along the narrow cardboard spines of his LP collection. He had been quite the rock and roller in his day and had even played in a band at one point.

"Aha!"

The old man yanked an album off the shelf. He reached inside and carefully plucked out the black disc. The vinyl shone under the lights above the turntable. Crouching down, Jared's grandfather carefully placed the record onto the turntable, fitting it neatly over the protruding piece of metal in the center.

"Sick record collection," Jared said. His own parents didn't own anything like this. They had a few CDs, but they mostly streamed music from the internet.

"Yeah, it's old tech," Jared's grandfather said, "but it's real." With great care he lifted a small plastic arm, moved it to the edge of the record and lowered it until the tiny needle was on the spinning record.

A scratchy drumbeat began to pump out of the speakers.

"What do you mean *real?*" Jared asked.

Jared's grandfather began swaying to the rhythm. Heavy bass guitar thumped along with the drums and was soon joined by the jangle of electric guitar.

"Come closer." Jared's grandfather beckoned, motioning to the disc in front of him.

Jared slid in beside his grandfather and stared at the record slowly spinning around. It was mesmerizing watching the lines on the black vinyl disc revolve.

"Today's music isn't real. It's all made digitally. A computer figures out a code for the sound, turns it into little ones and zeroes, and tries to make the best *copy* of what the music sounds like. But my record collection? It's all *analog*."

Jared shrugged.

"I figured that was going to be your reaction. But trust me, this stuff is fascinating! Analog is when a recording is made that's an exact duplicate of the actual sound itself." Jared's grandfather pointed to the spinning disc. "See that record?"

Jared nodded. "Yeah."

"It's really a series of grooves and pits. See that needle?"

Jared gave another nod, even though from his angle, he really couldn't see much of anything.

"The needle is diamond-tipped. It sits in between the grooves. As the height of those grooves changes, so does the sound. The sound perfectly matches the way it was created."

"And that's analog," Jared said. He didn't let on, but this was all pretty interesting.

"You got it, kid." By now Jared's grandfather was bopping his head and shaking his body. It was totally uncool, but Jared's grandfather didn't really care who saw him doing this.

Not caring about what other people thought of you? That was actually *for-real* cool. It suddenly occurred to Jared that his grandfather had been cool all this time.

So did that mean the music he was listening to was *also* cool?

If that were the case, maybe Olivia would be impressed too.

Either that or this thin mountain air was already getting to him.

Jared's head *did* feel a bit swimmy. Which was probably why he was seeing all those strange lights in the clouds through the giant windows across the room.

The lights seemed to be pulsing with the music on the record player.

Jared took a step away from the turntable and moved toward the wide windows.

The lights…

They were all sorts of colors: reds, blues, greens—every color in the rainbow.

Jared blinked.

The house rumbled slightly. It was a low vibration you might normally notice only deep in your gut, but this one was powerful enough to bump the needle off the record player.

For a moment all Jared could hear was the needle bumping over one of the grooves on the record, and the trail of scratchy static in its wake. *Bump. Rumblerumblerumble. Bump. Rumblerumblerumble. Bump—*

"Jared, get away from the window," his grandfather whispered. He sounded terrified.

Jared could not tear his eyes away from the lights. "But it's so beautiful—"

Just then a deep, resonant blast of sound blew out the windows, spraying fragments of glass across the wooden floorboards.

Jared was thrown back with the force and landed flat on his back. He looked up to see the turntable and the stack of records above it wobbling. He felt his grandfather's hands clutch his shirt and jerk him away.

A second later a huge stack of records toppled from the shelf and landed on the floor right where Jared's head had been. So did one of the wall-mounted speakers.

Jared heard his grandfather scream something, but it was impossible to make it out over the tremendous sound. It hurt his ears so much he had to clamp his hands over them. He barely had time to get to his knees when he looked through the broken windows and—

Something vast erupted out of the clouds.

The room was smothered in darkness.

Jared stumbled about, trying to find something to hold on to. The floor beneath him shook, and the rumbling in his ears increased. His mind raced. A plane perhaps? And those were its warning lights, and now it was somewhere above the house, maybe crashing. Maybe his head was filled with the roar of the jet, maybe these were his last moments alive, maybe—

Abruptly the sound ceased.

Jared was left standing in the dark, his ears still registering a high-pitched ring as if he'd been standing in front of live-concert speakers for hours.

And then...footsteps.

No. Something *like* footsteps.

The part like a footstep was the loud thump. It was the slow, dragging sound following each thump that set Jared's hairs on end.

Jared strained to see in the darkness. He rubbed his eyes and caught sight of a pair of silhouettes coming his way.

But silhouettes of *what* exactly? He struggled to make sense of what he was seeing.

They were living organisms, that much was clear. But Jared's brain was trying to assemble what his eyes were recording into something he could understand.

The two creatures that lumbered through the dark toward him and his grandfather didn't meet any of those criteria. They were blobby yet had some sort of constant substance, as if skeletons were holding their bodies together. But what kind of skeleton?

The creatures began to morph—or maybe they just came into focus. In just a few steps they went from being formless blobs to having limbs to having tentacles to having protrusions that made Jared's brain spin and his stomach turn. Processing their physical features demanded a clear head, and Jared's mind was awhirl.

One thing was clear. He had to run!

No sooner had Jared turned than he felt something jab him. He reached up and discovered a needlelike object dangling from his neck. He saw that his grandfather had been similarly punctured.

"Do not fear," one of the creatures said, although Jared didn't see much of a mouth—just a mass of writhing tentacles hanging off what he assumed was its face.

"You have been injected with a serum that translates our thought patterns into what you would call *language*."

Jared wrinkled his brow. "Huh?"

"You think you are hearing us, but in fact our thoughts are being transmitted telepathically to your brain. It is the easiest way we can explain ourselves without having to get surgical."

Jared opened his mouth to scream, but no sound came. His mind was still juggling too much—creatures that had no constant shape or form, creatures that had to be alien. Mind-controlling aliens at that. But what really freaked him out was the voice he heard. He could have dealt with the most gruesome, squelchy voices imaginable. What he couldn't deal with was an alien voice that sounded so familiar.

The creature spoke again, in an eerie parody of Jared's own voice. "You must leave this house at once, or you will be obliterated along with it."

"Obliterated?" Jared found himself saying, although he wasn't entirely certain his mouth had moved. If these things were communicating telepathically, was he doing the same?

But Jared's grandfather was shaking his head. "No, no, you can't! You can't take this house. Building it on this mountain has been my life's work."

"This planet is *mine*," one of the creatures said.

Jared was not sure which one had spoken. Then again, although his eyes had registered two life forms, who was to say they were separate entities?

"This *mountain*, as you call it," the creature continued. "You think it was created by wind and erosion."

"Yes, that's *exactly* how mountains are created," Jared's grandfather stammered. Even in this situation he was still a tough guy.

"Incorrect. This sphere you call a planet was put here by me."

Jared shook his head. "No, that's impossible. Earth has been here for, like, *billions* of years."

"That must seem like a great number of years to creatures such as yourself. *I* put this sphere here. I carved it out and made sure it could spin well."

"Spin well?"

"Every twenty-four hours the sphere rotates on its tilted axis. *Spins*."

Jared just stared at the creature.

"At 1,000 miles per hour. That's the speed required for the most desirable acoustics."

Jared's grandfather scratched his head. "Hang on a second. What do you mean, *acoustics*?"

"I mean, you primitive simian, that by using technology beyond the scope of your understanding, I have gathered debris from several corners of the nearby cosmos, spun them into this sphere you cling to for life and carved all the grooves and channels into it. Some of them were mountains like this one; others, great rift valleys and chasms. Some I filled with oceans so that I could create the greatest range of sound."

Jared tried to understand what this alien was going on about. These big ideas were making his brain feel like jello. So he tried to put it in terms he could understand. "Are you saying you *created* Earth?"

"Correct."

"And you built all the mountains and the oceans and, well, *everything*."

"Correct."

Now Jared's jello head was starting to spin. "To get the *right sound* out of it?"

The creatures standing before Jared and his grandfather shifted and blurred, and suddenly instead of two of them there were four. Jared felt his guts squirm. "It is, admittedly, an old technology," whichever one was talking said, "but one that reproduces sound the best."

Jared looked over his shoulder at the record player.

"It's the grooves in the planet, you see," the creature continued. "As it spins on its axis, the rise and fall of the planet's surface mimics the amplitude of one of our greatest songs."

Jared's eyes fell on one of the vinyl discs on the floor. He shook his head. "No. It can't be."

It was Jared's grandfather's turn to shake his head. "Can't be what, Jared?"

"Don't you see, Grandpa? This planet. Our home—it's just some alien record album."

The creatures shifted form, becoming a single tentacled blob standing before them.

"Yes. And you have gone and *spoiled* my sound by putting this infernal structure atop this protrusion. It's ruined *millennia* of work—which, I suppose might amount to your entire civilization's history. For me, though, it is an *extreme* annoyance."

"You're saying this is *our* fault?"

"You've raised the elevation of this mountaintop by ninety-two feet. It's thrown off the sonics throughout this entire range. I'm sorry, but it will have to go."

"My house?" Jared's grandfather yelled.

"Correct. In approximately eighty-three seconds, in fact. I would advise you to vacate the premises."

At this point Jared became aware of glowing red lights in the clouds. And a drastic rise in temperature.

He took his grandfather by the hand and ran for the car.

Eighty-three seconds later there was a massive explosion.

As they sped down the winding road, Jared and his grandfather watched the blaze through the side and rearview mirrors of the car. When they were a safe distance away, Jared's grandfather slammed on the brakes and flung open the driver's door. He staggered out of the car and dropped to his knees. "My house!"

Jared coughed some air back into his lungs, unbuckled his seat belt and spilled out onto the road too. He stared up at the blazing timbers and the black plume of smoke mixing with the cloud cover.

"It was your dream," Jared said, realizing the extent of his grandfather's loss. "And now it's all gone. Up in flames. I'm so sorry."

Though he was struggling to hold back tears, Jared's grandfather cracked the slightest of smiles. He even managed a chuckle. Then the chuckle grew into a giggle. Soon he was holding his sides and laughing so hard he could barely breathe.

"What?" Jared asked. "Why are you laughing?"

"Well," Jared's grandfather said, pointing to the shattered remains of his house, "that's rock and roll for you!"

BAD MOON RISING

"Don't worry," Hiro said, almost reaching out to put an arm on Liam's shoulder. He didn't, even though he could tell Liam was scared. Even though maybe Liam *did* need a hand on his shoulder. "It's only a drill."

Hiro could tell that Liam was watching their teacher, Mr. Reed, who stood in the doorway. Mr. Reed gave the hallway a quick scan and closed the door.

And locked it.

"Go to your safe spot," Mr. Reed said quietly, urgently.

"You've gotta be kidding me," Danielle snapped, eyeing the clock on her phone. "It's going to happen any second now."

"Seriously," agreed Nathan. He was holding a pair of sunglasses in his hands.

Everyone in the room had a pair of glasses like Nathan's, with thick, polarized lenses. Even Mr. Reed had been holding a pair, but he put his down on the table closest to the door and pointed at the students. "This is a lockdown!" he said a bit more forcefully.

"Lockdown *drill*," Nathan said, shaking his head. "How could they schedule one today?"

"Seriously," said Carter. He kept playing with his glasses, putting them on and taking them off. "This is the weirdest scheduling mixup in the history of scheduling."

"I know the timing is terrible, but it's mandatory," said Mr. Reed. "Please go to your safe spot like we practiced," he told them again.

Hiro agreed with Danielle. Why would the principal schedule a drill *now* of all times?

Most of the students did as they were told. But after a few minutes, Hiro noticed that some of them were slipping on their glasses and surreptitiously moving away from the safe spot in the far corner of the room and toward the exterior window.

Hiro kept his eye on Liam, who hadn't budged.

Liam had only been at the school for a few months, and Hiro still didn't know too much about him. He knew that he and his dad moved a lot—Liam hopped from school to school so often that he barely had time to make any friends. But Hiro liked Liam. It helped that they were both into skateboarding and that they both *sucked* at skateboarding. Liam had the scars to prove it. Hiro found it interesting that while Liam was never afraid to try out some crazy new skateboarding move, *this*, the lockdown drill, was freaking him out.

Liam whipped his head around. "Mr. Reed locked the door," he said. Apparently, he did not know what a lockdown drill was. Nobody else seemed to care. They were too busy trying to stare out the window at the sky.

"Didn't they do lockdowns at your old school?" Hiro asked.

But Liam wasn't listening. He was fixated on the door. He still wasn't moving toward the safe spot, so Hiro reached out and took him by the hand.

But Liam flinched and pulled his hand away. He looked absolutely terrified. "You don't understand. You can't understand. Even if I told you…"

"Told me what?"

Liam opened his mouth, about to spill everything. But then he noticed the kids by the window, hooting and nudging each other and playing with their special glasses. He shook his head. "We don't have time for this." His gaze went back to the door and the clock above it.

"Boys," Mr. Reed said sternly.

Hiro tried not to roll his eyes. It wasn't like anyone else in the room was staying put. They were all elbowing each other for a spot by the window, either staring out at the sky or playing on their phones.

"It's only a few minutes away," Danielle said. She had the special glasses on and was waving the rest of the class over. "It looks amazing!"

"Get away from that window," said Mr. Reed.

Hiro grabbed hold of Liam again and tried to drag him away from door. But Liam's gaze was firmly locked on the clock.

"There's barely any time," Liam whispered. He dug into his pocket and pulled out his cell phone.

"Who are you calling?" Hiro asked.

"My brother." Liam didn't look up from the phone.

"You never told me you had a brother."

"Yeah, well, there's a lot about me you don't know." He looked up at Hiro. "You need to get out of here," he said.

"You need to chill out," Hiro said back.

"You don't understand," Liam said. "It's *not* a drill!"

At the back of the room, by the open windows, excitement had begun to brew. "It's starting!" Nathan hooted.

"Don't look directly at it!" Carter chimed in.

About seven or eight other students were pressing so hard against the glass that Hiro wondered if the window might pop out under their weight.

"Eclipse selfies!" Danielle shouted. She held up her phone to record the image.

"Will you get away from that window?" Mr. Reed snapped, although nobody was getting away from anything. "It's against protocol!"

"Don't worry, Mr. Reed," Nathan said. "We won't look directly into the sun. We're not *idiots*, you know." He looked as if he was thinking something through. "Hey, maybe *that's* why we're having the lockdown. Because they don't trust us to not look at the sun."

"What do they think we are?" somebody else said. "*Morons?*"

Hiro was going to say something smart, but come on—it was the eclipse! How often did that happen? He didn't want to miss it.

Hiro moved away from Liam. He'd be fine for a moment or two. He reached into his pocket, pulled out his special sunglasses and made his way over to the window. He wedged himself between a couple of kids to get a good view.

"Isn't it supposed to go totally dark or something?" Danielle said, holding her camera up and taking some more snaps.

"Dark?" Hiro said. "That's only for, like, a few minutes." He turned to check on Liam, still over by the door. "Come on. Why don't you take a look, Liam? It's totally safe if you wear your glasses."

And then everything went dark.

The class started whooping and cheering. "Totality achieved!" Nathan screeched.

Hiro saw it, up there in the sky. The black disc of the moon blotting out the sun, only a flickering circle of light bordering it. It was unreal, like something from a movie.

"Amazing," he said.

And then he heard Liam pounding on the door.

"Come on, Liam!" he said. "We'll only be stuck here for a few minutes. You don't even have to look into the sun."

"Settle down, everyone," Mr. Reed hissed at the class, maybe at Liam. There was so much going on now that Hiro couldn't tell who was talking to whom.

Hiro moved away from the others by the window to make sure that Liam was okay.

"It's not a drill," somebody said—Hiro couldn't tell who. "There's somebody out there. Look!"

They were all pointing now, only it wasn't at the sun but at something running through the playground. A man but not a man. Nathan tore off his glasses and stared. "Is that…?" His mouth dropped open.

The class watched the figure approach the main doors.

Danielle screamed.

Instantly the bulk of the students tore themselves away from the window, leaping over desks or knocking into them and tripping over chairs to cower in the safe spot in the dark corner of the room.

And there was silence for the first time that day.

Only Mr. Reed stood by the window now, peering into the darkness. "What is it? What did you see?" he asked, his voice choked.

"It was hideous!"

"Some kind of monster!"

Everyone was talking at once.

Hiro and Liam still held their places by the door. "You knew this was going to happen," Hiro said, starting to piece it all together.

Liam, still facing the door, only nodded. "I'm sorry."

Hiro backed away. He had to get out of here. Get the keys from Mr. Reed perhaps. Get past Liam. Only now there was someone trying to get into the school.

From downstairs, even through the door, Hiro heard the sound of breaking glass. And screams. "What's happening?"

"My brother," Liam said. "He's not safe! He's only trying to help me!"

"What does he mean, *his brother*?" Nathan said, still cowering in the corner. "It wasn't even human."

"What?" Hiro said, but he could see from the look in Liam's eyes that Nathan was speaking the truth.

"I'm sorry," Liam said, looking first at Hiro and then everyone else. "Finn told me not to come today. He said the eclipse would make it happen. I didn't believe him. I'm sorry. I was wrong."

Liam hammered on the glass of the door. He turned to Mr. Reed and lunged at him. "Give me the key! You've got to let me out! You've got to do it *now*! You're in danger!!!"

"It's a lockdown," Mr. Reed said, his voice shaking. "We're all in danger." Hiro watched as Mr. Reed dug his hand into his pocket, probably checking he still had the key. "Liam, take a deep breath," he said. "This will all be over soon, and—"

Suddenly Liam dropped to his knees and started howling in pain. He clutched at his arms, his clothes, his hair, and began to scrape and scratch every part of his body. "Noooo!" he bellowed. "Not again. Not here!"

Hiro looked over at Mr. Reed. The rest of the class was silent. Liam had never gone into full-out crazy mode before, but there he was, thrashing around on the floor like an animal, kicking his legs so hard Hiro was worried they might come right off. One leg caught the edge of a desk and knocked it to the floor with a heavy thunk, spilling the contents across the floor.

"Liam," Mr. Reed said, his voice shaking with rage or fear—it was hard to tell which. He had put himself between Liam and the rest of the class. "This is a lockdown. It's not a drill. There is *somebody* in the building."

That shut everyone up. Liam moved from a fit of screaming to a series of gasps, like he was running out of air.

Hiro, the only kid not in the corner with the rest of the students, peered through the window in the door, trying to get a look down the hall, but it was dark because of the eclipse. Was there someone out there?

"We're going to get you out of here," Hiro found himself saying. "Just hold tight, Liam. Everything's going to be okay."

Liam, writhing on the floor with his head pressed against the cold tiles, gave a grunt. A low, deep grunt.

Hiro extended a shaky arm toward him. "Trust me, Liam," he said. "You're safe here."

"*But you're not*," Liam shot back, in a scary, distorted voice so wild that it made Hiro jump.

Liam's voice wasn't the only thing that was distorted.

It was hard to make out in the near darkness, but now that Hiro's eyes had adjusted, he could see tears along the seams of Liam's clothing. Like he'd burst out of them.

Liam stood up slowly.

Now Hiro understood. "Full moon," he said, or tried to say, but the words wouldn't come from his lips.

Liam stood well over six feet tall now. Thick, grizzly arms jutted far beyond the torn rags that had once been his clothing. His feet were now massive, elongated and sporting sharp, bloody claws.

The werewolf stood there, panting. Hiro looked into the creature's gleaming yellow eyes, searching for any sign of his friend. "Liam?" he managed meekly.

"Liam's not here right now," the creature uttered. It licked its muzzle with a long, pink tongue. From the pocket of Liam's tattered jeans, the creature produced a pair of polarized shades and slipped them on. "But don't worry. He'll only be gone a few minutes…"

THE LUNCHROOM

"We're not supposed to go in there," said Ali.

"Yeah, but come on," said Max. "Haven't you always wanted to see where the teachers eat?"

"Not really."

"Well, *I* do," Max proclaimed. He enjoyed proclaiming things. He shoved open the metal door, and in they stepped.

"Look at this place," he said, motioning around with his hand. "It's—"

"A boring room where the teachers eat," Ali finished. That's exactly what it was. The room was full of the kind of old furniture that most people would leave at the curb: a couple of tattered couches covered in stains, and a dozen or so mismatched chairs placed around a pair of long folding tables. On the counter at the back of the room sat a sad-looking microwave oven. Above it was a row of wooden cupboards. Beside it a faucet dripped steadily into the sink.

"Can we go back now?" Ali regretted having agreed to follow Max around on his weird little adventure. At first breaking into the staff lunchroom had seemed like a cool idea. Most things seemed like a cool idea when the alternative was working through questions from the social studies textbook. Mr. Dufrees loved textbooks. His class was full of them, and they were about as old and battered as the stuff in this lunchroom. "Mr. Dufrees will start wondering where we are."

"No he won't! He'll think we're in the washroom, like we said," Max snapped.

Ali looked at the clock on the wall. It was one of those old circular analog clocks. Why did schools even bother to keep them on the walls anymore? he thought. "We've been gone ten minutes already."

"That's because we're really, *really* constipated," Max said.

Ali peered around the room. "Remind me again why we're here?"

"Because we're going to find some dirt on the teachers," Max said as he started to move around the room.

"More likely we'll find dirt on these dishes," Ali joked.

Max was always looking for something ridiculous. He'd probably seen too many movies where the kids got the upper hand on their teachers and revolted. Ali figured that Max got bored easily and was entertained by that sort of thing.

Come to think of it, Ali also got bored pretty easily, which is why he'd decided that cutting out of class and breaking into the lunchroom was a not-bad idea.

Still, now that he was here, what was he supposed to do?

Ali opened the fridge. It was overflowing with plastic containers, a few half-empty bottles of sauce, and a row of milk and juice cartons that, judging by the rancid stench coming from the inside of the fridge, had clearly expired. Ali caught a whiff and coughed, then quickly shut the fridge.

Ali took another look at the clock. Max could stay here all he wanted, but *he* was heading back. Working on social studies questions was starting to seem much more appealing than hanging around a shabby lunchroom.

He moved away from the fridge and started to make his way to the door, then noticed the thing on the countertop.

At first Ali thought it was some kind of old cloth for wiping down the tables, one that had been left carelessly by a teacher or caretaker. But it caught his eye all the same.

Ali approached the counter and stared down at the cloth.

No, not a cloth, he decided.

Ali picked up the material, keeping it at arm's length. It was pinkish and soft to the touch. But it didn't feel like any fabric he'd ever worn. It felt more like…

"What's that you've got there?" Max asked. "Is it a dish rag?"

Ali hadn't been aware until now that Max was by his side, co-inspecting this strange new find.

"Weird," Max said. He took a corner of it and pulled it toward him. "It's not a rag. More like…"

"A *skin*," Ali said, his voice choked to a whisper.

A skin, yes. Like the kind that covers a human's body. This one was about the size and shape of a head. A real head, with holes for the eyes and ears and nostrils and—

Ali stopped. A hole where the *mouth* is.

Instinctively he let go of the thing. As it dropped to the floor, he let out a yelp and wiped his hands on his shirt. *What had he touched?* It wasn't warm like his own skin, but it had the same texture, the same stretchy give.

A mask maybe? That was the only explanation he could think of. But Halloween had come and gone. And why would there be one here in the staff lunchroom, of all places?

"I don't like it," Ali said.

"Yeah, but we came here looking for cool stuff, and guess what we found? Cool stuff!" Max picked up the mask from the floor, put it in front of his face and started making weird animal sounds through it.

"Stop that," Ali said.

Max lowered the mask. "Oh, come on, Ali. This thing is neat."

"Let's go back."

"But we're having so much fun," Max said. He rolled the mask up into a ball. "Think fast!" he told Ali and hurled the mask his way.

Ali ducked. The mask sailed over his head and hit one of the cupboards at the far end of the room, causing it to creak open.

"Cut it out, Max!" Ali snapped. Fear had given way to frustration.

Then Ali saw Max's expression shift. He was looking past Ali, at the open cupboard, and saying nothing.

"What? What is it?"

Ali turned. And then he *saw.*

What should have been in the cupboard was kitchen stuff. Stacks of mismatched dishes. Cups. Random coffee mugs.

But instead there were masks. Rows and rows of masks, arranged with purpose and hanging on hooks. There were also rows of skins to cover arms and hands.

And wigs! Ali spotted the set of red curls he saw every day on Miss Miller's head and the wispy gray strands he'd mistaken for Mr. Dufrees's actual thinning hair.

Ali tried to decide whether to run now while the going was good or get to the bottom of this mystery.

Curiosity won out. Why the masks? "For *all* the teachers?" he wondered aloud. "All of them? They're all in on this?"

"Sure looks like it," Max said. He was breathing heavily now.

Ali gulped. "But wait. Your *dad*'s a teacher. He works over at Bonder Public at the other end of town."

"That's exactly right, Ali," Max said. He dropped another mask he'd pulled out from the cupboard. It fell to the floor with a wet slap.

Only now did Ali realize that Max had put himself between Ali and the door—the only door to the lunchroom.

Ali recoiled. It was some kind of weird, sick joke. Max loved weird, sick jokes, and he was playing one on Ali now.

In backing away from Max, Ali bumped into the wooden cupboard where the teachers presumably kept all of their dishes and cutlery.

Cutlery.

Ali turned and yanked open the closest drawer.

Knife.

There was no thinking involved.

Grab a knife. Defense. Escape. That was all that coursed through the reactive part of his mind, a blind survival instinct already kicking in, here in the staff lunchroom, of all places, with his best friend.

But there was no knife in the drawer. Only more of those skins.

Faces. *Masks.*

Ali's stomach rolled and twisted until he was sure it was in the misshapen form that this collection of faux-human skin was.

"Why do you think I brought you down here?" Max said, moving closer.

Ali didn't respond. He threw open another drawer with such force that it clattered to the floor. Marbles spilled out and rolled across the linoleum tiles.

Marbles?

No, not marbles.

They were spherical, but they were all uniformly white, with circular designs on each one.

Eyeballs.

Not real, of course, and that's what made his skin crawl.

No cutlery. No forks. No spoons. The room wasn't a lunchroom. It was a dressing room. Skins and hair and eyes.

Ali tried to move out toward the door, but he slipped on the eyeballs and fell to the floor with a thud, landing face-first in the mess of horrid orbs.

He pushed himself back onto his knees, but Max was standing over him, leaning in close.

Ali could see that Max was still breathing heavily, but the breaths weren't coming from deep within his chest. The sides of Max's neck were swelling and deflating as if he had gills.

He pulled at his neck, and the skin covering it began to come away, revealing a slick surface underneath. Dark and oily and covered with scales.

Ali's gaze moved from the scales to the flaps of skin hanging from Max's face. His skin was loosening around the eyes, around the nostrils and, yes, around the mouth. He'd been wearing a mask himself this whole time? A long, slender tongue snaked through the opening of the mask, where Max's mouth should be. It was yellow and forked and curled like some kind of proboscis.

"C'mon, dude," Max said. "This is a lunchroom. And I'm feeling really hungry."

In the distance, a long, sustained bell rang.

The lunch bell.

FLOATERS

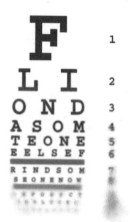

When I woke up on Tuesday morning something was different. But what? Everything in my bedroom was just as it had been. The same toys were strewn across the floor. The pile of laundry in the corner was just as high and, yes, just as stinky.

I tried to figure it out as I got dressed. I didn't feel any different, which I'd been expecting—a scratchy throat or a stuffy nose. Nothing like that. And when I stole a glance at myself in the mirror on my wall, I didn't *look* any different either.

Still, something was wrong.

I saw it only when I went to brush my teeth and snuck a peek at myself in the mirror. There it was.

A *squiggle*.

A see-through squiggle. At first I thought someone had drawn it on the fogged-up mirror, but when I went to wipe it away, the squiggle *moved*. I looked left, and the squiggle glided off the mirror and to the wall I was staring at. But it wasn't on the mirror or the wall. It was floating in the corner of my eye.

I scanned the pale tile walls of the bathroom, and the squiggle followed my gaze.

I thumped downstairs. Mom and Dad were frantically getting ready for work. Only Grandma, who lived in our basement, was moving at a regular pace. She chomped down on a plate of sausages. The squiggle in my eye got lost in the view. I explained everything to her.

"Oh, that's just a floater," my grandmother said.

"A floater?"

"I'm old, and I've got plenty. They look like little worms, don't they? Or cobwebs. Or clouds."

I shook my head. "Mine's just a squiggle in the corner of my eye."

Then Grandma leaned in close, so it was just her stale breath in my face and her shaky voice in my ear. "That's how it all starts, my dear."

"Don't get him started," my mother said. She handed me a bowl of cereal. "You probably didn't get enough sleep, Michael. That's all. You'll be fine in no time."

Mom was usually right.

But not today.

As I walked to school, I noticed a couple more floaters slowly slip into my field of vision, making a total of three.

I shifted my glance to the sidewalk. When I looked down, the floaters were lost among the cracks and bumps in the pavement. But every time I craned my neck up to the sky and took in its deep-blue hue, the floaters emerged, snaking across the view.

Where had they come from? Had they always been there, buried in my eyeballs like a nest of wriggling maggots?

"Hey, Michael!"

I blinked, and the floaters reacted. They squirmed around in my field of vision.

"Michael, you okay?"

I blinked a few more times and looked up to see Devon, who I always met up with just outside the school grounds. He and I had been best buds since kindergarten.

"I've got floaters," I told him.

He gave me a look. I explained what my grandmother had told me, that as the body ages, you build up little squiggly things in your field of vision. Like me, he found it hard to believe. "Yeah, that's your grandma talking. We're not old, Michael." He thought some more about this. "Maybe you were staring at the sun for too long."

But I hadn't been.

"And you can still see them now?"

I stared at Devon, and the floaters inched around my eyes. I took a deep breath and tried to figure out if I could actually feel them moving like they were alive.

Blinking didn't help, but maybe washing out my eyes would. That was the first thing I did once we got to school and the bell rang. I made a beeline for the washroom and doused my face with water from the sink. I stared at the white ceiling tiles, hoping the floaters would be gone from my field of vision.

No good. The little wrigglers were still there. I could see through them, like they were transparent, but they kept squiggling and moving about, making it hard to focus on any solid color for too long.

I wiped my face and went back to class. Maybe I had to tell my parents. Maybe it was something I needed to go and see a doctor about.

But first I had to get through the day. At least they weren't hurting me. They were more like an annoyance, these little bits of wobbly jelly that came into focus whenever I stared at something static for too long, like the whiteboard or the blank page of my notebook.

That's exactly where I was staring when I saw the floaters moving again, only this time—

I gasped.

They were twisting and turning like they were alive.

Only this time they were forming letters.

HOW IS LLOYD DOING?

That's what they spelled.

I tried to blink the floaters away, but when I closed my eyes, Lloyd's name just stood out more brightly.

Lloyd? *Lloyd Matheson?*

I glanced over my shoulder. Lloyd was sitting way at the back of the class, his head tucked down in a book.

I looked back at my book, and even though nothing was written on the blank page, I could still see the floaters, and that's what they wanted to know. How Lloyd was doing.

I turned back to Lloyd, my breathing uneven.

Lloyd was quiet. Lloyd kept to himself. I had barely ever spoken to him, except for the day before during our math activity. Mrs. Estevez had paired us together. I'd done all the work, and all Lloyd had done was stare at me.

Stare at me.

I started to get out of my desk, but the recess bell went off, and everybody burst out of their seats.

By the time I'd pushed through the crowd of classmates making their way in the opposite direction and edged toward Lloyd's desk, he was gone.

"Come on, Michael!" Devon called from the front of the room. "I need to kick your butt at wall ball."

"You go on ahead," I told him, still hanging around Lloyd's desk.

Peeking inside his desk, I pulled out his notebook and opened it up.

I turned pages, past all the notes he'd taken from the whiteboard over the past few months, until I reached a blank one.

Except it wasn't exactly blank. Lloyd had scribbled in the date on the page—yesterday's date, to be precise.

And he'd scratched something else in his book in squiggly letters. It almost looked as if he'd been drawing the same kind of weird formations I'd been seeing in my eyes.

Capital letters.

FIND SOMEONE ELSE, they spelled out.

I turned the page.

FIND SOMEONE NOW.

I turned the page again, but this one was blank.

"Michael?" a voice called out.

I looked up. Mrs. Estevez was at her desk, arms crossed. "You want to stop snooping through other people's work and get outside? Or do I need an actual reason to keep you in?"

I shook my head and shoved the book back into Lloyd's desk. "No, Mrs. Estevez, sorry," I said, my voice choked.

I hurried outside before she could say anything further.

The schoolyard was beyond busy. In the few hours between coming here this morning and now, it seemed as if we'd imported about a thousand more students.

And I was only looking for one.

Finally, after ten minutes or so of searching, I found him.

Lloyd was way at the edge of the field, standing against the rusty chain-link fence that bordered our playground. The wind had swept all sorts of plastic bags and litter against the fence, and they fluttered in the cool breeze. Beyond the fence was a field of overgrown weeds and, past that, the rest of the subdivision.

I started heading his way.

The bell rang for us to come inside, but I didn't care. Neither, it turned out, did Lloyd. And the fence was so far away from the school that no teacher was going to see us. I'd have a few minutes before our absence was noticed and we were called inside.

"Hey, Lloyd?" I called out when I thought I was close enough for him to hear me.

He didn't turn around.

"Lloyd?"

I kept pressing forward, until I was only a few feet away from him.

"It's happening to you now, isn't it," he said without even looking at me.

"Huh?"

"They get into you through your eyes. That's how they pass from person to person. If you stare long enough, they find a way in."

"What are you talking about?"

He turned and stared at me, and I stepped back.

Before today, Lloyd's eyes had been blue. After all, he'd been staring at me with those blue eyes intently all day yesterday. But now, they were just...

Just black. Like something had scooped out the color from them. Scooped the color—or eaten it.

"It's the floaters," Lloyd said, shaking.

In the corner of my eye I could see the squiggles changing, shifting. Forming new letters...

"They travel from person to person. I didn't know that then, but I know it now. They get into you, and they move from person to person. I got them from my cousin. He got them from his friend."

The floaters shifted. I turned my head to the blue sky above me, and I could see the letters.

FIND SOMEONE ELSE, they said.

Lloyd put his hand on my shoulder. His arm was so thin, I realized. He'd been a pretty solid guy once, but now he seemed almost skeletal. His cheekbones were poking out of his face, and his eye sockets were sunken and hollow. He opened his mouth, and all he could manage was a wheeze. "They're telling you to do something, aren't they?" he said.

I nodded.

The cold wind blew, and Lloyd took his arm off my shoulder, hugging himself to keep warm. "We've got to get inside," he told me. "We've got to find a cure. But until then you've got to do what they say. Or else they'll take more than just your eyes!"

"How?" I managed to ask.

"Find someone and look them in the eye. Unless you can think of a better way to pass them on."

So we went back inside, and I thought about it.

And I'm very sorry, dear reader. Very, very sorry. But there's only one person whose eyes have been open for long enough.

Long enough to read these words, in fact. It's *YOU*.

It was all part of my plan, you see. I know it's not fair, but as Grandma says, since when is life fair?

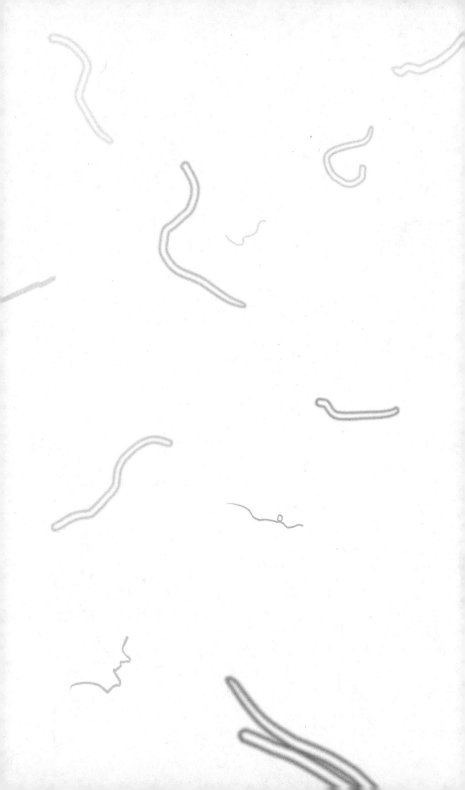

YOU CAN SEE THEM NOW, CAN'T YOU?
WHEN YOU CLOSE THIS BOOK
AND STARE AT SOMETHING
FOR LONG ENOUGH,
YOU MIGHT CATCH
ONE IN THE CORNER
OF YOUR EYE.
EVEN FOR JUST A SECOND.

ALL I CAN SAY IS, WHATEVER YOU DO,
MAKE SURE YOU FOLLOW
WHAT THE LETTERS SAY.

GOOD LUCK.

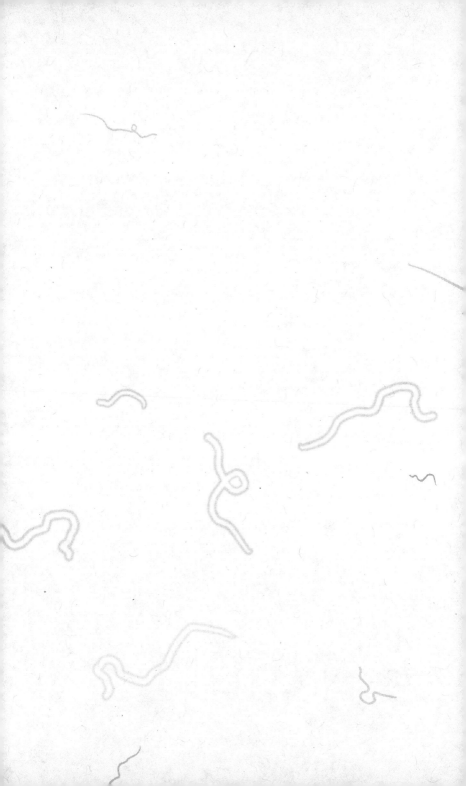

ACKNOWLEDGMENTS

I've been a lifelong fan of the classic, scary episodes of *Dr. Who* and writers like Roald Dahl, Douglas Adams and Richard Matheson. I bet readers who are paying attention will see some hat-tips to these masters reflected in this collection of stories. You wouldn't be reading them without the collaboration of the amazing people at Orca, including Tanya Trafford, who went the extra mile to help bring them to spooky perfection. And Steven P. Hughes continues to astound me with his incredible art.

Of course, none of my books would be possible without the support and commitment of my wife, Danielle Saint-Onge. Thank you as always.

But I must also acknowledge the dark spot in the corner of my writing room. It talks to me as I type these words.

It says it wants me to thank it as well, that I would be nothing without it. I tell it *No*. I tell the dark spot that it can't actually speak, that in fact it doesn't even exist, that it's just a shadow in the corner of my office. The dark spot says I have made it very angry and then tells me it's going to show me how much it actually exists, that it's going to take me over…

I say, *NO! No, dark spot!*

Dark spot…

Nooo….ggghghhhhhfjjgkgll;;;;

…..

DARK SPOT SAYS JEFF WILL LISTEN TO IT FROM NOW ON.

DARK SPOT SAYS YOU WILL ACKNOWLEDGE IT TOO.

DARK SPOT WARNS YOU TO HEED IT SO YOU DON'T END UP LIKE JEFF.

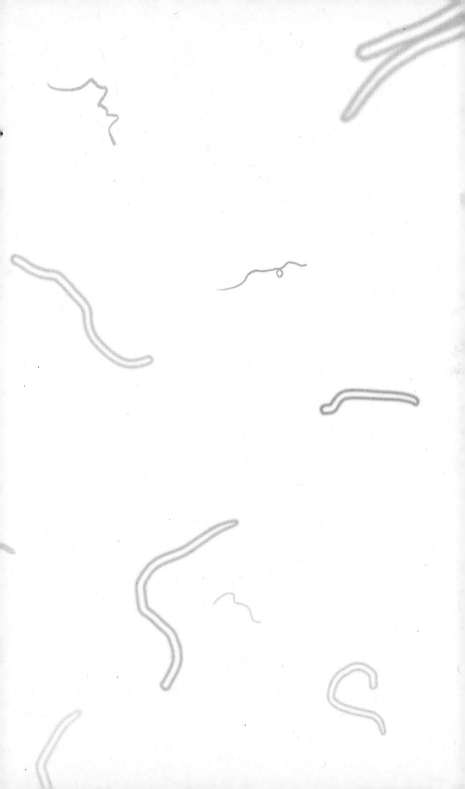

JEFF SZPIRGLAS is the author of several works of fiction and nonfiction, including the horror collection *Tales from Beyond the Brain*, the best-selling *Wild Cards* and the Red Maple Award nominee *You Just Can't Help It!* He has worked at CTV and was an editor at *Chirp*, *ChickaDEE* and *Owl* magazines. He is the father of twins and has two cats (the cats are not twins). In his spare time, he teaches second grade. Jeff lives in Kitchener, Ontario.

STEVEN P. HUGHES is a horror enthusiast and award-winning Canadian illustrator of several books, including *Tales from Beyond the Brain* and the graphic novel *Tru Detective*. When not drawing, he enjoys spending time with his wife and their two dogs.

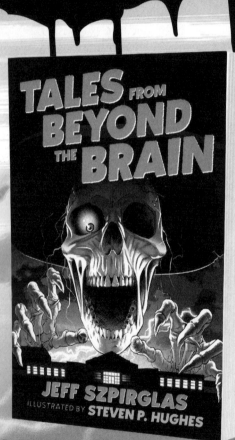